TO FORGIVE BUT NOT TO FORGET

MARION CATTERALL

DIAMOND MEDIA PRESS CO.
1-747-998-2352
https://www.diamondmediapressco.com/

ISBN Paperback: 978-1-951302-269

Contents

About the Author vi

About the Books ix

Acknowledgements xi

Chapter 1: The Final Goodbye 1

Chapter 2: Starting Again 7

Chapter 3: Chance Meetings 15

Chapter 4: Love Rekindled 29

Chapter 5: Reconciliation 55

Chapter 6: Married 65

Chapter 7: The Manor 81

Chapter 8: Sir Arthur 115

Chapter 9: Final Commitments........................135

ABOUT THE AUTHOR

Marion Catterall lives in the northwest of England and was educated at the Convent of the Holy Child Jesus in Preston, Lancashire. She started a few stories back then but never finished because life got in the way. However, she has now written and published three novels and is completing her fourth. She is very excited and pleased by the reviews she has received. For years she ran her own haulage business. She is married and has children and grandchildren.

ABOUT THE BOOK

To Forgive but not to Forget tells a standalone story in the same milieu as its predecessor book, *Let Love Be My Judge.*

Jilting her fiancé only a few weeks before their wedding, Catherine elopes with a different man. Then she loses her husband. A chance meeting with her jilted fiancé results in the rekindling of their previous, tempestuous relationship. The descriptive sexual content in this book demonstrates the love, desire, passion, pleasure, and emotion of the situations she finds herself in. A romantic, erotic love story.

ACKNOWLEDGEMENTS

To my dearest husband, William; my two sons, David and Stephen; and my three beautiful girls, Jennifer, Clare, and Sarah – with all my love and affection.

CHAPTER 1

The Final Goodbye

It was early in the morning on a very rainy May day. It must have been about two o'clock when I looked out the window of the hospital room to see if I could watch the world passing by. All I could see were the droplets on the glass, reflecting lights from vehicles.

I turned to look at Thomas Hague, my beautiful husband. He was lying peacefully in the hospital bed, attached to all sorts of weird and wonderful machinery. In one arm, he was attached to a blood transfusion drip, and in the other arm, he was attached to a cocktail drip of cancer drugs.

He looked so handsome. He had always been so handsome: tall, good physique, dark hair, dark skin, beautiful dark eyes. He looked as if he were just asleep. He was not asleep; he was in a coma.

I had lost all sense of time. I was in a living nightmare, and I could not wake from it. I was desperate for Thomas to wake up. "Just one more time, please, let him wake up."

I whispered those words over and over. It was my prayer.
I wanted to look, into his eyes. I wanted to tell him how much I loved him. I wanted to tell him that I would love him forever and a day. *Please, please let him wake up just for a few moments before he leaves me forever.*

I could not cry. I felt so numb. I wanted to scream and shout, "Thomas, Thomas, for my sake, wake up. Wake up!"

I sat back down on the chair by the side of his bed. I didn't know how long I had been sitting on that chair. I put my head on his pillow as I held his hand. I whispered in his ear, "I shall never forget you. I shall always love you. Please always be with me. Keep your arms around me and hold me tight. I need to know that you will never leave me. Please open your eyes just one more time."

As I lay there, I recalled our wedding. We had eloped to Vegas eighteen months previous. Both of us had, had weddings booked for the following month of December. Thomas was to marry Susan Johnson in Los Angeles, and I was to marry Squire Donald McFadden in Scotland.

Thomas and I were scheduled to marry people we did not love enough. We did not love them enough because our feelings of love, affection, and respect were for each other. We knew we could no longer keep living a lie. We knew we could not live without each other. We made the decision to elope to Vegas, marry immediately, and enjoy our lives together for all time. In reality, "For all time," meant around eighteen months or so.

A nurse came into the room. "Mrs Hague, why don't you go home and get some rest? If there is any change in your husband's condition, we will contact you straight away, and you can make your way back here."

"No, thank you. I need to be here in case he wakes just one more time, so I can look, into his eyes."

"If you insist on staying, I will bring you a sandwich and a hot drink. You must promise to eat and drink them. You have to keep your strength up," said the nurse as she left the room.

I lay back down on Thomas's pillow. I closed my eyes as I remembered Thomas and I leaving the Little White Chapel on the Vegas strip. At last we were married. We had been given the use of a large wedding limousine for the day by the Vegas Tourist Department.

As we entered the limo, Thomas said to the driver, "Wedding breakfast at Lake Meade followed by a drive through part of the canyon, please, driver."

"Yes, sir, and congratulations to you both," replied the driver.

We settled down in the backseat, holding and kissing each other. "Well, Mrs Hague, how do you feel?" asked Thomas.

"I feel wonderful, Mr Hague," I replied with glee.

"I don't know where we are going to live. I don't know what we are going to do from now on. One thing I do know is that we shall always be together. We will survive anything from now on," remarked Thomas.

As we drove away from Vegas, Thomas looked at me and said seriously and quietly, "Before we start our married life journey, we have to make two unpleasant but important phone calls. I suggest we do this now, in order to move on."

I agreed. In the silence of the back of the limousine, Thomas phoned Susan Johnson. The conversation was short and to the point. After explaining the circumstances, Thomas offered to pay all costs for the cancelled December wedding. Distressing but done.

Then it was my responsibility to phone Squire Donald McFadden. Donald was a force to reckon with. He was larger than life, a blond, tall, handsome Scotsman in his mid-forties. The laird of the Thistle Isles, he was also known as the Squire Donald McFadden and was the current head of the McFadden clan.

Donald answered his phone. My heart was pounding so loudly I could not hear anything else around me. I told him about my marriage to Thomas, that it was not premeditated, and that I had no intention of hurting him, but it was what it was.

I remember the long, deafening silence that followed. Donald said, "Do you know what you have done, Catherine?"

"Yes."

Speaking very precisely, Donald said, "You have betrayed me. You have betrayed the McFaddens. No one ever betrays the McFaddens without some restitution. You will pay for what you have done. No matter where you are, I will make sure that you never get away with what you have done to me. Mark my words, Catherine. I will get my own back on you!"

I was so frightened and upset that I turned my phone off. Distressing, but job done.

The nurse returned, bringing me a sandwich and a hot drink of tea. As she changed the fluid bags and made Thomas more comfortable, I slowly drank the tea. I made my way back to the window. Dawn was breaking and the rain had stopped. I could see people going about their business and vehicles driving everywhere. I knew that once Thomas left me, my life – my world – would never be the same. At that moment, I felt I would never be able to cope with a future without him.

When the nurse left, I returned to my chair. Before I sat back down, I kissed Thomas on the lips. I blew breath on him, just as we used to do in our intimate moments. I sat down, and again I put my head on his pillow. As I looked at Thomas, I recalled some of those moments. We loved each other so much, the intimate side of our relationship was always brilliant. Was there really life after death? Who could answer that for me?

The door opened, and in came Justin, Thomas's brother. Thomas was part of a large family. The Hague family was also The Hague Corporation, a company which owned several large golf resorts, hotels, and spas. Most were in America, but after they purchased a considerable amount of land from Squire Donald McFadden in Scotland, they built a huge golf resort there.

"I have come to sit with Thomas for a while. Why don't you go home for a few hours, Catherine? I will contact you if there is anything to report," said Justin quietly.

"No. Sorry, I will not leave him. He might open his eyes one more time. I need to talk to him."

"He will never come out of this coma now. We just have to wait for him to die. The blood cancer has made his body close down. Nobody can do anything to stop him from dying." Justin sobbed those words out. He just stood there and cried. I could not console him because I could not console myself.

Justin, his wife, and other members of The Hague family had helped Thomas and I start a new life after we eloped. They helped us find and buy a beautiful house in Santa Barbara, which we made into a home – our home. They helped Thomas secure a directorship in The Hague Corporation. They helped me adjust to the American way of life. I was introduced to some fascinating people, and I made some really good friends.

But where were they when I needed them? Obviously, they were getting on with their own lives. Thomas and I were both in our forties. We had made many plans for a future together. Once Thomas left me, I would have no future.

"I have made arrangements for a priest to come and administer the last rites to Thomas. I hope you agree," Justin said.

I nodded. I looked at Thomas, knowing Justin had given up on him ever regaining consciousness. I had not given up. *Please, please, Thomas, open your eyes and look into mine,* I prayed silently.

An hour or so later, the Catholic priest arrived. He wasted no time in administering last rites. As the priest anointed Thomas's hands and head and prayed over him, I felt angry at the whole situation. Why? Why? Nothing made any sense.

The priest asked Justin and me to join him in prayer. I could not. I did not want to. I wondered again, *Is there life after death?* No one really knew the answer to that question. What a waste of time.

Not long after the priest had gone, a doctor and a nurse came into the room. They removed the drips from Thomas's arms. They did not replace them. Some of the monitoring
equipment was turned off. The drip stands were taken away. Thomas's white top sheet was removed and replaced with a clean, crisp, blue top sheet. They spoke to Justin and me very quietly. I didn't know what they said. All I knew was that Thomas was leaving me and he was not coming back.

He never did open his eyes.

C H A P T E R 2

Starting Again

As I left the hospital on that dreary morning, I was numb. I walked slowly to the taxi rank. I watched people rushing past. Everyone seemed to be in such a hurry.

When I got into a taxi, I could not remember my home address. The driver helped me look through my purse, to see if my address was written on anything. Once he found it, he drove me home. I paid him and walked up the entrance steps to the back- kitchen porch.

I was met by Annie. Annie had been Thomas's housekeeper for many years. He once told me that she might be his housekeeper but she was also his best friend, his confidante, his personal assistant and much, much more.

I loved Annie as much as Thomas did. I did not need to talk to her; she knew that it was all over. Again, I could not comfort her as she cried and cried. I could not shed a tear. All I felt was anger.

I had not slept for days, so I made my way to our bedroom. I lay on our bed and stroked the bedding on Thomas's side. We had loved and cuddled every night in that bed. I drifted into a deep sleep. I wished that I would never wake up – that somewhere in my dreams, I would find Thomas waiting for me.

It was the day of Thomas's funeral. All The Hague family had rallied round me, and they had made most of the arrangements. I was feeling more like myself. I was in control of everything around me. Though I felt as if I were in full control, it all seemed to be a bad dream, and soon I would wake from it.

When I entered Thomas's study, my attention was drawn to a picture on the wall. It was a card that had been framed many years ago. The image was of a little cartoon girl and boy waving goodbye to each other. Each had a tear near their eyes.

I had sent Thomas that thank-you card as I was leaving America and returning to England. I had asked him to always keep his arms around me and always hold me tight. That had been a long time ago.

When Thomas phoned Annie and asked her to empty his safe and prepare him a bag of clothes so he could leave quickly and in secret, he had also asked her to pack the framed card. I knew that I must never be parted from that picture. I would treasure it forever.

Dressed in a beautiful grey suit with a pale blue blouse underneath, matching grey shoes, and a large blue-and-grey hat, I sat in the funeral car. Then I walked behind Thomas's coffin into church.

I looked around the pews at all the people who had come to say their last goodbyes. Most of them I did not recognise, not that I was bothered. Nobody mattered to me anymore! My children, Carol, Jennifer and Tony, were unable to be with me on this sombre day. My children were from a wonderful first marriage. Their father died. In fact, nobody from my family were able to make the long journey, but they had all said that their thoughts and prayers would be with me. Poppycock, I thought. No one had any idea of the loss I was feeling. Of the injustice of it all. I felt so angry!

As I stood at the graveside, many people were crying. I watched Thomas's coffin be lowered into the ground, and I could not cry. There were no emotions left in me. I was relieved when it was time to go home.

A reception had been arranged at one of The Hague Corporation's hotels. I left them all to do what they wanted to do and made my way home alone. I curled up on our bed, and then I prayed to Thomas.

"Never leave me, Thomas. I need your arms around me. Please do not let me down," I whispered into his pillow.

The next twelve months passed quickly. I was happy with Annie in our home. I occupied myself by getting involved with some of The Hague Corporation's projects. I had inherited Thomas's shares, and these shares provided me with a decent income.

Only a small amount of my time was spent with The Hague Corporation. I entertained friends, and I travelled all over America. I was quite capable of travelling on my own. I always met some great travelling companions.

I was lonely. I considered myself to be quite attractive. I was tall, slim, and had blonde hair and green-grey eyes. I met many men, but I never met a man who set my heart beating. Apart from Donald McFadden, no one could thrill me like Thomas had.

I was not bothered if I never found another man to get close to. If it was going to happen, it would happen. I knew that Thomas would not expect me to go through life without the love of a good man.

It was not long before I realised that I needed to be in England. I had many friends and family there. America had been kind to me, but I needed to start a new chapter in my life. I needed to be near my children and grandchildren and all my close friends.

Annie wanted to retire and move away to join her family. Now was the time for me to sell up and move back to England. There was nothing to keep me in America.

I made the decision to sell the house. I left everything

in it, apart from Thomas's picture. I made sure that I kept it safe among my personal possessions. As I held the picture close to my heart, I still could not shed a tear. I had never cried for the loss of Thomas. Only anger was in my heart.

My family agreed that I would stay with my daughter Carol, until such time as I purchased a property for myself.

With all the goodbyes said, especially to Justin and his family, I made my way to the airport. As I boarded the plane, I felt as if I was deserting Thomas. I had never felt as lonely as I did at that moment.

Within hours I was arriving at Carol's house. My other daughter, Jennifer, had arrived as well. It was wonderful to have all my family around me. Tony, my son, phoned me to welcome me home. He was away travelling.

That night, as I lay awake in the guest room, I knew that I had to start to make some concrete plans for my future. Even though children love you, they really don't want you to move back into their lives.

Before I left for America to be with my beloved Thomas, I had lived in northern England, just south of the Scottish border. I had relatives there, especially my sister Margaret and her husband Matt. I also had close friends – Sarah, Judith, and many more – living within a few miles of my previous house. I had enjoyed being part of a golf club as a committee member.

I had also lived near to Donald McFadden's stables. I loved to go riding with him. I was quite a good horsewoman. Donald also frequented my golf club when he stayed at his Lancastrian estate.

All well and good looking back on how it used to be. I knew that I could not just move back where Donald could reach me. I felt uneasy at the prospect of ever meeting Donald McFadden again.

He owned two estates. One was near Lancaster and the other, his seat, was in the Isles of Thistle. He resided there at Heatherfield Country Manor, and on his land there was a restored castle.

I had lived with him at the manor on occasion, but never on a permanent basis. Our last serious break-up had occurred because he had a woman named Sheila Jones living on his Lancastrian estate while I was living with him at Heatherfield. He was always telling me that he would sort it. Fool me, I believed him.

His family, especially his mother and the elders of his clan, had great hopes and expectations for Donald to settle down and marry Sheila Jones. She was younger than I was. I was a mother and a grandmother. I presumed they all hoped that Donald, one day, would have an heir.

Donald loved me, but he also had a great appetite for women. He was determined to marry me against all odds and against his family's instructions. We were a month away from our wedding day when I left to find my true love, Thomas Hague.

For me to settle back in England, I needed to be well away from where I used to live. I knew I had hurt and betrayed Donald, but it was done now. My friends Sarah and Judith had kept in touch with me. They told me that Donald had married Sheila Jones and that they had a little boy. I wished him well. I was too wrapped up with the loss of my beloved Thomas to worry or care about anything or anybody else. I was really struggling to come to terms with my loss. I had tried counselling, but it did not alter the facts and the situation.

I was an emotional wreck. I felt like I was on a hamster wheel, constantly going around and around. At the same time, I was going deeper and deeper into a really, dark, bad place. I could not help myself. Sometimes I wanted to go to sleep and never wake up. Perhaps I would meet Thomas in my dreams.

While I was staying with my daughter Carol, I spent a considerable amount of time looking for my own house. I searched the Internet until at last a promising house came on the market. It was situated in a small village not far from the coast. It was quite a few miles away from where I had used to live, but still in easy reach of my friends and relatives.

I arranged a viewing. From the first time I entered that house, I knew it was the perfect place for me to make a home.

It was a large, detached, Georgian, double-fronted house. It had large gardens and a beautiful drive leading up to the pillared front porch and door. There were five bedrooms, all en suite; a beautiful kitchen; lounge; and dining room. I did not need to do anything to it. It was picture perfect.

Within two months I was moving in. I had plenty of help from friends and family. Once settled, complete with new furniture and soft furnishings, it was time for everyone to leave me on my own to try and get my life back.

It was not long before I started to feel really depressed. I was lonely. Apart from a housekeeper who worked for me three times a week, I did not want to meet anyone at all. I knew what was happening to me, but I could not seem to do anything about it. I missed Thomas so much.

Shortly after I had moved into my new home, I received a call from Justin, Thomas's brother. "How is my favourite sister-in-law?" he asked.

"I am fine. It is lovely to hear from you!" I exclaimed. "What can I do for you on this lovely day?"

"Business and pleasure, I am afraid. You know that there is an Annual General Meeting, coming up and it is to be held at the Thistle Golf Resort and Spa in Scotland. Well, of course you know that. You have a responsibility, as owner of Thomas's shares in the corporation, to be present and to vote on all the issues on the agenda. I thought that Elizabeth" – that was his wife – "could make the trip with me, and that we could all meet up and stay at the hotel together. Elizabeth is really excited at the whole idea. What do you think?" "Sounds wonderful. Yes, it really does sound wonderful," I answered.

"I will e-mail you the itinerary and book you into the hotel. All you have to do is turn up. It will be next month. Is that still OK for you?"

"Yes, yes, fine. I am really looking forward to it!"

When the call ended, I was surprised to find that I really was quite excited at the prospect of seeing Justin, his wife,
and other members of Thomas's family.

I received the e-mail from Justin. All that remained was for me to get myself sorted out with a complete new wardrobe, from shoes to suits to accessories. Perhaps that was what I needed to help lift me out of the bad place I was in.

I really enjoyed preparing for my trip. I also started to enjoy my new house. I became good friends with my housekeeper and looked forward to a better future.

My housekeeper, Mrs Hilda Hargreaves, was the same age as I, and she lived close to my house. It was a comfort to know that she was going to come to the house at certain
times. Having someone to talk to made all the difference to me.

I decided to have a radical haircut. Very short was the order of the day. I smiled at my courage, but I was really pleased with the way I looked.

There was one large downside to my excitement: the risk of meeting Squire Donald McFadden. Donald had once owned the land which the resort was built on, and used not only the links, but the restaurant and bars.
I would do everything in my power to avoid him. I was so afraid of his reaction if we were to meet.

CHAPTER 3

Chance Meetings

I took the train to Edinburgh and then a taxi to the hotel. Case in hand, I made my way cautiously into the reception area, hoping that Squire Donald McFadden was nowhere around. Success! I booked into my room and was relieved when I opened its door with no nasty incidents to report.

It was a beautiful room, complete with a small balcony that overlooked the golf course. I made my way to the fridge bar and helped myself to a large brandy.

It was not long before Elizabeth, Justin's wife, phoned me from their room, and within minutes she was joining me with a brandy. It was lovely to meet her again. We had a closeness, as sisters-in-law, that I needed and appreciated.

Funny though – nobody ever wanted to talk about a deceased person. They probably thought that I would break down and cry if they were to mention Thomas's name. How wrong they all were. I had no tears inside me.

The meeting went as it was meant to do. No problems. It was wonderful seeing everyone I knew from America. It was proposed that I be offered a formal position in the corporation, as a representative resident in the UK. Specifically, I was offered the management of the Thistle Resort. The vote for this was unanimous, and I gratefully accepted. I knew that there was no hurry to start, and I was surprised at how excited and positive I felt about it, even though it meant that I would probably have to re-think where I was to live.

Elizabeth and I went out to the shops. We dined at lunchtimes in bistro bars, and at night we all went out to the larger restaurants in the area, mainly Chinese restaurants. That suited me, as there was less chance of meeting Donald.

"Have you any problem with us dining here at the hotel for our last night, Catherine?" asked Justin. "I am aware that you have some reservations about perhaps meeting Squire McFadden."

I laughed and answered, "No. Obviously, I do not want to come into contact with him, but I will have to face him at some time. I will miss you and Elizabeth. I wish you were not going home so soon."

"Why don't you come over and spend some time with us and the children? Perhaps next month. Come and stay for a few weeks. We would really love you to come," said Justin. Elizabeth hugged me and said that she would not take no as an answer. I agreed to meeting them, in the near future.

On the last night, we booked into the resort's restaurant. I made sure that I looked especially good. Why? I had no idea why.

When we had finished the meal and were saying our goodbyes, I noticed Donald in the adjacent bar. I watched him for a little while. My heart was pounding. He looked so handsome. As usual, he was surrounded by his male friends and also by women desperate for his attention. Nothing new there. I used to call his women followers "clucking hens".

I smiled to myself as I recalled the clucking hens from his past. Donald was a charismatic man. He had once been a very eligible bachelor, so he had a great following of beautiful young women, all of them desperate for his attention. Yet Donald had loved me and looked forward to us getting married.

I made sure that Donald could not see me. I was afraid of meeting him, but I enjoyed watching him. In fact I got quite a thrill from watching him. I recalled how much we had loved one another once.

I said, "Justin, if you speak to Donald, please do not tell him that I have been here with you all. I would rather he did not know."

"I understand. We will not say anything. But you will have to meet him at some time if you are taking on your new position here."

"I agree with you, but not tonight. I am not ready to meet him yet."

Our goodbyes said, I made my way to my room. I could not sleep. I kept thinking about Donald and, of course, Thomas. Thomas had left me and was not coming back, but Donald was still there.

I was angry with myself for feeling excited when I watched Donald. I remembered how I had felt when Donald touched me. I recalled the feelings I had had when we kissed. I re-imagined the wonderful sex we had had together. I felt so guilty!

I was relieved when I left the hotel the following morning and returned home.

It had really been good for me to go to Scotland and meet up with Justin, Elizabeth, and other friends. I knew that was the way forward for me. I had to start getting out, meeting new friends, involving myself in new projects. The position at the golf resort was just what I needed. When was I to take up this new position? I did not know. I was not quite ready.

I was greeted by Hilda, my housekeeper. "Before I forget, your sister Margaret has been asking for you. She wants you to phone her as soon as you are rested up."

As Hilda brought me some tea and sandwiches, I phoned Margaret. "Lovely to speak to you," Margaret said. "I thought I would give you something to arrange to keep you occupied. There is a party of fifteen of us, relatives and friends that you have not seen for some time, and we would like you to arrange a New Year's holiday outing. The majority of us would like to do Scotland and Hogmanay, but I am not sure how you would feel about that considering your own personal circumstances?"

"Yes, I can arrange that. I will make sure that we are miles away from the Thistle Isles." We both laughed.

It was a joy making the arrangements for a New Year's holiday together – not only Margaret and her husband, Matt, but long-time friends and a few cousins as well.

I decided to make it a glorified coach holiday. I booked a coach that would take us to a Scottish castle. As long as I stayed well away from the Thistle Isles, all would be well. I decided on a hotel in the northernmost part of Scotland. *Yes, that will do nicely,* I thought. The coach would take us sightseeing during the day. Maybe we could go whale watching or look for seals in the small harbours. A week away in Scotland would be something special for us all.

I arranged and booked it all. We would arrive the day before Hogmanay. Brilliant; I was already looking forward to it.

When the time arrived, however, I was not so impressed with the idea of being in a hotel in northern Scotland in the middle of winter with Margaret and the others. How boring was that going to be? I knew that a few of the party were single, so I would not be on my own in not having a partner.

I tried to excuse myself, but Margaret was having none of it. I decided to get on with it and take the holiday as it came. Perhaps I would enjoy it.

On the departure date, the private coach collected each guest, and before long we were heading north on the motorway. It was a long journey. Even though we had several comfort stops, by the time we arrived at the hotel, we were all completely fed up and very tired.

The hotel resembled a Scottish castle but was not in fact a historic building. Still, it looked very impressive and authentic. It was situated on a raised concrete platform. A large patio surrounded the whole of the building. The patio was flagged and enclosed by wrought-iron fencing. On each side of the hotel, large, wide stone steps went down to the landscape gardens, all of which were snowy white with the frost and light snowfall.

Each of us was thrilled by our rooms. Some of us were lucky to have a four-poster bed. I was not so lucky, but the views from my windows made up for it.

After an evening meal, we retired to our beds. We were all exhausted. I had a good hot bath and went straight to sleep, not waking until the morning.

The next day was New Year's Eve, Hogmanay in Scotland. It was a leisurely day. I made use of the time by exploring the hotel and the grounds. Then I prepared my clothes and accessories for the night's celebration.

Everyone in our party were dressed in evening wear: the women in gowns and the men in dinner suits. What a handsome bunch of people we were.

After the evening meal, we took seats for the dancing. There was a small annex to the large ballroom which was perfect for our party. It had a long table that would seat us all, and although we were not actually in the ballroom, we had an excellent view of the dance floor, stage, and roaring fire.

"Come on, Catherine!" shouted Margaret. "You can sit yourself here at the end of the table. I know you don't want to be near the dance floor." I agreed and made my way into the corner, away from the main ballroom.

There was much laughter as everyone tried to get a good seat. They finally settled down, ready to enjoy the night's entertainment. Drinks were ordered, and the compere for the evening introduced himself.

"Margaret, I am going to the ladies' restroom. Please make sure that my drink is placed here," I shouted.

"I will, but please do not be long, or you will miss something."

I made my way to the restroom, which was situated in a corridor away from the ballroom. The corridor led on past the restroom to the large entrance doors at the front of the hotel.

I wandered around and watched as several Scotsmen, all wearing the full Scottish outfits, exited the building. I could hear the wind howling outside. I presumed that these men were preparing for the firework display at midnight.

I entered the ladies' room and reapplied my make-up. I checked my dress and was very pleased with the way I looked.

As I left the restroom, I glanced towards the entrance doors. A tall Scotsman, wearing all the Scottish garb, kilt and the like, walked briskly in my direction. I stopped to admire his outfit and his long, bright, yellow, weatherproofed coat. Oh! My goodness! It was Squire Donald McFadden walking towards me!

A second later and I could see that he had recognised me. He continued walking at quite a fast pace. All of a sudden, he had his arms wrapped around me, pushing me up against the wall. His lips were heavy on mine. As he kissed me, I could feel his tongue touching my lips, my tongue. There was such urgency in his kiss.

I put my arms around his shoulders and kissed him back. I could not catch my breath. The sensual feelings pleasured my whole body.

Donald whispered, "Are you in a relationship?"

"No. Are you?"

"I don't know. I am in the middle of a divorce; does that count?" Without pausing for an answer, he added, "Whose bed are we in tonight, mine or yours?"

I was taken aback by that question. I did not know how to answer him.

"For goodness' sake, Donald, we need you out here. Please hurry up!" shouted a man outside the door.

Donald moved away from me. "Answer me, Catherine – mine or yours?"

By this time, more than one person was shouting to Donald. They were getting pretty angry.

Although I had a room to myself, I told Donald that I could not offer my room, as I was sharing with another woman. I thought that would get me out of the strange situation I had found myself in.

"So, it is my bed then?" said Donald.

I did not answer. I was still trying to understand what was happening.

"Catherine, yes?"

I nodded. Donald ran down the corridor, shouting back that he would come and find me later.

I was in shock. I returned to the ladies' room, where I sat myself on the sofa that was there. I was still feeling the aftermath of Donald's kisses.

I thought about Thomas. Only Thomas had ever made me feel so good sexually. I missed Thomas. He was always in my thoughts. I was finding it hard to get on with my life while I was constantly thinking about him and missing him so much.

My sister entered the ladies' room. "There you are. What have you been doing? We are all waiting for you. I was getting worried."

"I am coming now. Sorry!" I said. I got up and made my way back to the seat that had been chosen for me.

I drank my drink with a blank mind. I could not think straight. I watched the cabaret and really enjoyed the pipers. I did not say anything to Margaret as I did not want her to fuss and worry over me. I had to learn to stand on my own two feet.

On this occasion, I felt I had no option but to spend the night with Donald. I was very excited at the prospect. It was not long before Donald appeared in our little annex.

He walked over to our large table and, with a beautiful smile on his face, addressed our party. "I hope you are enjoying the atmosphere here. My name is Squire McFadden, and I wish to welcome you to this hotel and our Hogmanay celebrations. I will arrange for a bartender to come and take your order for drinks, on the house. Is there anything else I can help you with?"

"Yes, Squire, there is!" cried Lillian, a friend of my sister.

"Fire away. What is it?"
"We all want to know what is under your kilt!"

Everyone around the table laughed. Donald replied, "Oh, my dear, I am so sorry but it is forbidden for me to tell you. I can assure you that it is all in good working order."

The whole of the table laughed again with glee. Donald walked over to me and offered his hand. I accepted, and we walked out of the annex and onto the dance floor. As we walked away, Donald turned and said, "I am just taking Catherine to show her what is under my kilt." This time, even I laughed.

Once on the dance floor, Donald held me close. I had nothing to say to him. I just wanted to enjoy the feeling of closeness and the sexual thrills raging through me.

"Donald, I am sorry, but I am not going to spend the night with you," I whispered.

"Yes, you are." He held me closer than before.

"You must listen to me. I am not in a good place at the moment. Did you know that Thomas died?"

"Yes."

"It would be unfair of me to go to your bed tonight. I would most certainly let you down. I feel as if I am on a wheel that is turning, going deeper and deeper into the depths of I don't know what, and I cannot get off it. I feel so guilty about you and I. How can I have sex with you with this guilt hanging over me?"

Donald made no effort to reply. He walked me off the dance floor and out of the ballroom, into a small, quiet lounge. "Sit there and do not go away! I shall bring us some drinks." He left the room.

I thought, *What am I to do? The last thing I want is to be reunited with Squire Donald McFadden. But the thought of Donald touching me sexually sends shivers down my spine. It feels so wrong. My heart is heavy with guilt.*

Donald returned and gave me a glass of whisky. He sat on a chair near mine. Neither of us said a word. As Donald drank, he looked me up and down. He focused on my breasts, then my eyes, and then back on my breasts. It was exciting. It had been such a long time since I had wanted a man to hold and love me.

As soon as we had finished the drinks, Donald explained that he was to help with the midnight firework display.

"What are you doing here, so far from the Thistle Isles, on such an important night as Hogmanay?" I asked quietly.

"Each year the clans take turns in providing the Hogmanay celebrations. This year it is here. Why?"

"I was concerned that I was not prepared to meet you again, so I chose a hotel miles away from where I thought you would be. That didn't work, did it?" I said, half-heartedly laughing.

"Fate has a strange way of making things happen. I suggest you bring a good warm coat down here and leave it in this room. After the New Year has been let in and everyone is preparing to go outside for the fireworks, collect your coat and make your way outside. I will find you. Happy New Year, Catherine."

With that, Donald got hold of me and helped me to stand. With his arms wrapped around me, he kissed me, and I kissed him back. Wow! There was no denying the attraction we had for one another.

Donald left. I collected my warm coat and, as he had suggested, left it in the small lounge. Then returned to my party's table. I helped myself to a drink that had been left, and I drank it all.

My sister Margaret was watching me. She knew what had been happening, and of course she recognized Donald McFadden as soon as she saw him. "Be careful, Catherine. Donald McFadden might be out to hurt you, if not physically than maybe emotionally. Do not trust him."

Midnight approached. I collected my coat, wrapped myself up, and went outside. I stood beside one of the large front pillars. It was warmer there. The fireworks display was magnificent. But I was not watching the fireworks – I was watching Donald walk up and down the firework line. He was laughing with his co-workers. He looked so tall and handsome. I also noticed several women watching him.

As he had said, Donald found me shortly thereafter. "What did you think of the firework display?"

"Brilliant," I answered.

"Do you want another drink or maybe a dance? Or will you come with me to my room?"

"Take me to your room."
Donald put his arms around me and led me up the large staircase. Neither of us said a word.

When I entered Donald's room, I was pleasantly surprised to find two large whiskies and two hot coffees waiting for us. It was as if he had known that I would agree to come to his room sooner rather than later. I smiled at that thought. The cheek of him!

As I sat at the small table, Donald said, "I do not want you to bring guilt into our relationship. You have nothing to feel guilty about. If you had not done what you did, I would not have my baby boy Jack. He is the reason I wake up in the morning. He makes life worth living. He is nine months old now, and I get to have him stay with me most weekends. He was to stay in this bedroom tonight, but I wish to be with you tonight. My mother has him sleeping in her room.?

"Does your mother know why you want her to have her grandson tonight?"

"Well, not really." He laughed.

Before I had finished my coffee and brandy, Donald had started to take off his wonderful Scottish clothing. "Do not worry. I will not rush you. Neither will I expect you to do anything you do not want to do," he said.

Yet I stood to remove my clothing, slowly, item by item. I could see that Donald was extremely excited. When we were both naked, I walked over to him and pressed my body against his. I was just as excited as Donald seemed to be.

We kissed and kissed. Donald caressed my body, paying particular attention to my breasts: stroking them, holding them gently, squeezing my nipples hard. We then lay on the bed, and it was not long before I felt the penetration of Donald's penis. Thrills rushed through my body as Donald moved with precision. I felt a wave passing over me and knew something good was going to happen. Sure enough, I climaxed with energy and felt Donald ejaculate.

With a sheet wrapped around us, we lay holding each other tightly. The afterglow of that beautiful lovemaking lasted. Then Donald whispered, "Why? Why could you not have loved me as much as you loved Thomas Hague?"

Thank goodness the telephone rang. It was his mother to say that Jack would not settle, so she asked Donald to collect the baby and bring him back to this room.

"I must go now," I said. "I have loved your lovemaking, and I have loved holding you tight." I quickly dressed and headed for the door.

"No. Do not leave!" said Donald.

"I will not stay in your room with you and your baby son. Sheila would kill you if she found out, not to mention what your mother would do. Trust me. I know!" I hurriedly left.

Back in the sanctuary of my own room, I reviewed what had happened to me that night. Was it all for real? Would Donald and I get back together? Would there be a future for us together?

I climbed into my own bed and fell fast asleep.

CHAPTER 4

Love Rekindled

I awoke very early that morning. *New Year's Day,* I thought. *What will happen to me in this newyear?*

I could still feel the glow of Donald's lovemaking. I could not believe how much I loved having sex with him. Even more surprising was the fact that I had no trouble responding to his lovemaking. I had some decisions to make on this beautiful, cold, and crisp morning. Would I walk away from Donald forever, or would I rekindle our previous love affair?

It was far too early to make such life-changing decisions. After a good hot shower, I dressed in my warmest clothes, put some make-up on, and set off for a walk. I had no intention of turning up for breakfast in the dining room. So many nosey people would stare at me. Worst of all, I would have to face Donald's infamous mother. Ugh. A lovely walk was far preferable.

I walked for a long time. Returning to the base of one of the large entrance steps, I heard my phone rang. "Hello?" I answered.

"Where are you? Your presence was missed at breakfast, and not just by me," Donald said lightly.

"I took myself for a long morning walk, and I am now on the steps that lead to the hotel. Which set of steps, to which side of the hotel, is anybody's guess."

"I will bring you a hot coffee. Don't worry; I will find you. Take your time ascending those steps. I will see you at the top – maybe about lunchtime?" Donald laughed.

I took my time climbing the icy steps. Soon I could see Donald at the top. He was holding his small baby son. Actually, I should say that he was holding his large baby son. Obviously, the baby took after his father. I smiled at that thought.

Donald gave me the coffee and introduced me to Jack. He was so proud of him.

"He is beautiful, Donald. His curly blond hair and striking blue eyes are quite a giveaway as to who might be his father," I remarked as I touched the baby's hair.

All of a sudden, from around the corner, Donald's mother came towards me. She was shouting at me, blue in her face from rage. "How dare you! Have you no shame? Don't you dare touch my grandson! Why have you sought out my son? You must know he is happily married. Shame on you! Leave him alone, or you will have me to deal with!"

Donald tried to interrupt her but she would not be silenced. Eventually, Donald said, "You are out of order, Mother! In case you had forgotten, Sheila and I are getting divorced. We are far from happily married."

Mrs McFadden took hold of Jack, turned to Donald, and said, "Sheila has moved back into the manor. She has halted all the divorce proceedings. We are all ready to go now, so I suggest you leave this woman and take us back to where you rightfully belong!"

With that, she pushed past me. Donald said, "I know nothing about what my mother said. I have to go and find out what the bloody hell is going on!"

I stood drinking my coffee as Donald rushed away. I thought, *Nothing has changed. I am still answering to what Sheila wants, and Donald is still trying to please her as well as me. Not this time though. I have no intention of resuming any relationship with Donald under these circumstances.* As far as I was concerned, my heart and my soul were still very much with my beloved Thomas. I did not need or want anybody else.

I had a brilliant day. Our party was treated to a fantastic sightseeing excursion. When we returned to the hotel that afternoon, I was pleasantly tired and looking forward to a good evening meal. Later, there would be entertainment in the ballroom.

Just as I expected, the evening meal was delicious. Casually dressed, I joined Margaret, Matt, and most of our party in the ballroom for the evening entertainment.

At the interval, the compere set about doing a quiz – a quiz with a difference. The answers to the questions had to be the most outlandish answers the participants could make up. It was the most comical thing I had done for a long, long time. I laughed out loud.

"Right, ladies and gentlemen, please be on your best behaviour, as we have royalty in the room!" said the compere. "Welcome, Squire. Would you like to play along with us?"

I froze when I heard those remarks. I looked over to the bar. There was Donald, toasting the compere with his drink. The compere resumed his quiz, and I continued to participate in it. I just acknowledged Donald with a nod of my head. He was surrounded by his man friends and his clucking hens. Nothing new there.

As the evening's entertainment recommenced, Margaret said, "Cather ine, I think Donald is trying to get your attention. Has he come back for you? If he has, please be careful. I do not trust his motives. He will end up hurting you."

"Don't worry. I can take care of myself. Let's be honest: nobody else is here to take care of me – apart from you and Matt," I hastily added.

I walked over to the bar, past the clucking hens, to where Donald stood. He immediately held me tight and kissed me. "I am so pleased to see you. I presume we are in my room tonight!" he whispered.

"You presume too much. If what your mother said is true, then under no circumstances will I be at your beck and call. I will never come second best to Sheila again. I think you might have wasted your time with this return journey."

Donald pushed me to the corner of the bar. "Right!" he said. "Don't you ever speak to me with that condescending tone again! Whatever happens to me does not give you the right to threaten me. Do you understand? I am going to ask you a question, and I want an honest answer from you."

I nodded, though I felt quite uncomfortable about the way he was speaking to me.

"Forget everybody and everything that is happening around us. Just me and you; nothing else matters. All I want to do tonight is hold you close. I want to kiss you and make love to you. Now for the question. Tonight, do you want me to hold you tight? Do you want me to make love to you? I need an honest answer from you, just a yes or a no."

I started to say something to him, but he stopped me and said, "Yes or no. Don't try my patience! Well?"

"Yes," I whispered.

Donald put his arms around me and kissed me ever so gently. "Chef is making a meal for me. I have not eaten all day. I am very tired, so I will go to the dining room now and I will see you later. Is that all right with you, Lady Catherine?" He smiled as if he was laughing at me.

"Whatever you want, Squire!" I replied. We both laughed.

I returned to Margaret and told her that I was to stay with Donald again that night. "Do not worry about me. I know exactly what I am doing."

Sometime later, Donald joined us and made polite conversation with Margaret and Matt. We then made our apologies and headed straight to Donald's room.

That night, we held each other tight. We kissed and made love as lovers do – that is, with an urgency as if we were to part. We could not get enough of each other.

As we were drifting into sleep, Donald said, "My car is full of clothes, computers, riding gear, office files, and of course my passport and personal papers."

"You have left the manor?"

"Yes. I am to leave here tomorrow morning, early. I will take up residency at the Gables. I can run the estate and stables from there. I will not be returning to the manor until such time as Sheila has left. I have already spoken to my solicitor and instructed him to start divorce proceedings on my behalf. He will also apply for my custody, either joint or full, for Jack."

The Gables was a large Georgian house on Donald's estate near Lancaster. It was when he was living there that I had first met him quite a long time ago. It was situated not far from my new house.

"Do you still have a housekeeper there?" I asked.

"Of course!"

Very early the next morning, Donald woke me to say goodbye. I did not know what to say or do. We kissed and then he was gone. I lay there wondering why I was feeling so sad. I had experienced a feeling of total loss for Thomas, and somehow I felt similarly when Donald left me with no mention of any future contact.

The week 's holiday was a great success, but I was pleased to be back home. I greeted my housekeeper and friend Hilda with all my tales and stories. I even told her about my time with Donald.

"That week 's break in Scotland has done you a power of good. You seem so uplifted. I presume you are on your way to becoming the woman you were before Thomas died. Perhaps you can start the process of moving on," she commented.

I was shocked that she thought that way. "I will never get over Thomas leaving me. It is not time for me to start thinking about other relationships. How could there ever be anyone else for me?"

"I apologise if I spoke out of turn. I do hope that one day you will meet someone. I just thought that because you spoke kindly about Donald that—"

"Yes, you do speak out of turn! Perhaps I should not have told you about the squire."

"I apologise again, Catherine, but please remember this: it is never the one you haven't met – it is always the one you can't forget." With that she left the room.

Several weeks passed. I had not heard from Donald. I kept myself busy, preparing for my new employment at the Thistle Resort. I had spoken many times to Justin, and he confirmed that I need not take up my position as general manager until I was ready to do so. The position did not call for hours and hours of work. In fact, according to Justin, I was only an overseer, and a visit every few months would suffice.

As time went by, I started to look forward to taking up the position. I would stay at the hotel and meet all the friends I had previously made there. It was not long before I finally, made a decision, to book into the Thistle Resort and arrange an induction day.

A few days before I was to travel to Scotland, I was driving near the Gables. I decided, on the spur of the moment, to call and see Donald to tell him of my new position.

I parked in front of the Gables and rang the bell. I was nervous. The housekeeper answered the door and explained that Donald was not in. She told me that if it was important, I would find him at the stables. She started to give me directions, but I thanked her and told her I knew the way.

I got back in my car and wondered if I had the courage to go to the stables. Not really, but I decided to go for it. The car park of the stables was not far. It brought back memories of when I used to go riding with Donald.

I got out of my car and walked into the stable yard. Goodness, nothing had changed. I saw a stable girl and shouted to her, "Is the squire around here today?"

"Have you come to go riding with me?" Donald called back from one of the large stable blocks.

"Of course! Unfortunately I have forgotten to bring my riding gear," I answered merrily.

It was so good to see him again. I watched him walk across the yard towards me. My heart was pounding and my hands were clammy.

"Not a problem! Ann, take Lady Catherine to the tack room and kit her out – OK?" he said, looking straight into my eyes. He had always called me Lady Catherine when I used to frequent these stables, oh so long ago. The sexual attraction between us was undeniable. "Well, go with Ann and let us see what you can do after all this time."

"Now hold on, I only called to see how you are and to tell you that I am to do a little work at the Thistle Resort. I thought you might be interested."

"Could not give a damn! I am more interested in you coming for a ride with me now. Go on. Get changed, and hurry! I do not have all day."

With that, I followed Ann into the tack room and found suitable riding gear to change into. I then met Donald in the yard. Within minutes a horse was brought out of the stable block, already tacked up. Donald offered me his hands to throw me up and over. Once I was mounted, he himself brought his large horse out. Off we went through the farm gate and into the field beyond.

Riding next to Donald felt good. We laughed and joked. Donald led the way into the trees. At the other side of the wooded area, we rode towards the river. There, Donald stopped, dismounted, and helped me to dismount.

As his arms went around my waist, I shuddered with sexual feelings. Within seconds his lips were on mine. I put my arms around his shoulders, pulled him into my body, and kissed him back. The sensual thrill was so honest. We kissed and kissed. We touched each other provocatively.

I was not sure where this was going, so I thought it best to calm the situation down a little. "How are you?" I asked, trying to get my breath back.

"Why do you want to know?" retorted Donald. "What really brought you here today, Catherine?"

"Honestly, I wanted to tell you about my new venture as overseer of the Thistle Resort. I am going there next week and will stop a few days at the hotel."

"Have you missed me? Have you given me a second thought? Do you daydream about you and me making love?"

"Yes, I have missed you, and I have thought about you often. I just don't know what I want. I still feel so lost, and sometimes I feel depressed." Inside, I was really insecure.

"Come on. We had better get back before they send a search party out for us. I have people coming to the stables this afternoon, and I really don't want to be late," said Donald.

We rode back, chatting and laughing again. I enjoyed the experience. All too soon, we were back in the stable yard.

Ann, take Lady Catherine to the tack room. Bye, Catherine. It was good to see you." Donald walked back into one of the stable blocks.

I changed as quickly as I could and wasted no time in making my way back to my car. I found a business card that I had recently had printed. It noted my address, telephone number, and email address. I asked Ann to give it to the squire. I then drove away.

My heart was still pounding. Why had Donald been so cold to me when we returned to the stables? I wondered if he recalled the day he abused me in the tack room. It had been a long time ago, but I certainly remembered that awful afternoon. We had so much history between us.

I also remembered what Hilda had said to me: "It is never the one you haven't met – *it is always the one you can't forget.*"

A few days later, Donald at last came to see me. I was pleased to see him, and he seemed equally pleased. He greeted me with a friendship kiss and appeared more interested in looking around my house and garden than in looking at me. "This is truly beautiful, Catherine. Your choice of a new home was very good. I was passing and thought you might fancy going for an Indian meal tonight. There are a few of us meeting at the restaurant. Do you fancy?"

"Yes, please! I have not had an Indian meal for a long time. I would love to come," I replied.

"Good. Pick you up at seven!" he said and made a hasty retreat to his car.

I spent the rest of the day preparing to go out with Donald that evening. I knew that I was feeling much better about myself than I had done a few weeks earlier. I had loved Donald once – but that had not been enough to stop me from marrying Thomas Hague. Now I seemed to be falling for Donald all over again.

Seven o'clock came. Through my open front door, I saw Donald's white Mercedes turn in to my drive. I also saw a woman in the front passenger seat.

I closed and locked my front door. Donald met me and opened the back door for me. "Catherine, this is Pauline," he said as he closed the car door. "Pauline, this is Catherine."

As we drove off towards the Indian restaurant, Pauline said, "Do you have an interest in horses, Catherine?"

"No, afraid not," I politely replied.

"Don't let her fool you, Pauline. Catherine is a very good horsewoman," Donald said.

I moved towards the centre of the backseat so that I could look at Donald in his rear-view mirror. I caught his gaze and made a really screwed-up face. He rewarded me with a wink. He always made me feel so good.

"Do you like Indian food?" asked Pauline.

"Yes, but I must admit, it has been a while since I have been out for an Indian meal."

"Oh, Donald and I go out for an Indian meal once a week. Don't we, love?"

Donald nodded, and I suddenly realised that I did not know him well at all. It sounded to me that Pauline and Donald might have some sort of relationship going on. I felt sick.

When we arrived at the restaurant, Pauline did not let go of Donald. We met the other people in our group, and introductions were made all round. I knew a couple of them, but not well. I was seated next to a lovely man – a farmer, I believe. Pauline sat on my other side, and Donald was seated next to her. I could not even see him.

The evening was wonderful. The company was great. Stories and jokes were told. There was laughter, and the food was brilliant. Everyone seemed to have a great time. When the meal was over, we were escorted to a lounge to await coffee and liquors.

I saw Donald holding Pauline's hand as they walked from the dining table to the lounge. I was quite shocked. Why did I feel so jealous? Jealousy was an emotion that I had not felt for a long time.

I realised that all the feelings I had had for Donald in the past were still there. In fact, I was more attracted to him now than I had been before. I had Thomas Hague on my mind and in my soul, all the time, but Donald was here for real.

I excused myself and made my way to the ladies' restroom. A few of the ladies in our party were there, and Pauline came in shortly after. I busied myself with freshening up.

One of the women asked, "Catherine, are you the one who was due to marry Donald a few years ago?"

I saw the horror on Pauline's face. "Yes." I replied and made no effort to elaborate on that answer.

The other women left to return to the lounge area, but Pauline stayed behind with me. "Are you and Donald more than just good friends?" she demanded.

"Sorry, I think you need to ask Donald that question. It is for him to answer."

I returned to the lounge and sat near Donald but on a different sofa. Pauline sat next to him on the same sofa. "When do you go to Scotland, Catherine?" he asked.

"Sunday or maybe Monday," I replied. Without thinking, I added, "Come with me, Donald. You can catch up with your mates and your colleagues – even your clucking hens. I shall make sure we have a really lovely room. The days could be yours but the nights would be ours. It is only for a couple of days, longer if we want. What do you say?"

Donald made no comment. I felt defeated but I knew that it served me right. I had been full of my own feelings, not taking note of the people who were around me.

I ordered a double whisky and waited until the time to be taken home.

I climbed into the back of Donald's car again as Pauline seated herself in the front passenger seat. I did not take much notice of our route until Pauline remarked, "Are you taking me home first?"

Donald replied "Yes, sorry. I am staying with Catherine tonight."

When Donald stopped outside Pauline's home, she got out of the car, slammed the door, and ran up her drive. Donald drove away. "Catherine, are you OK staying in the rear seat? We shall be at yours in a few moments."

I could not believe my luck. I knew that I must not spoil this chance to find some happiness with Donald. That is, if it was meant to be. "Are you stopping with me tonight?" I asked.

"No. If we are leaving for Scotland the day after tomorrow, I have a thousand and one things to do first. I also have some conditions before I actually agree to come with you."

"Go on, then. Tell me your conditions," I said smiling at him.

He parked in my drive and opened the rear door for me. "I do all of the driving," he said.

"Yes."

"We use this time together as a honeymoon practice."

"Yes."

"You agree to marry me when my divorce is through."

"Yes."

My heart was pounding, my hands were sweaty, and I was so overcome with emotions I did not know whether to laugh or cry.

Donald held me tight. We kissed goodnight. "I still love you, my Lady Catherine. Goodness knows why. I will never let you down, but you must never let me down. Do you understand what I am saying? I am not joking. From now on, it is you and me and a life together."

"I am so happy. I thought I had lost you as soon as I found you again.

Please, please be patient with me, Donald. I have so many demons that I have to deal with. I still feel so guilty. I will do my best to make you happy. I am falling in love with you all over again."

"Go on, go in now. I will pick you up Sunday morning, bright and early. Our future starts here and now." Donald laughed as he slipped back into his car.

He did not wait until Sunday to see me. On Saturday evening, he came with a Chinese takeaway and a bottle of wine. The car was already packed for the journey.

With the fire lit and music playing in the background, we enjoyed the wine and the takeaway. The restful atmosphere and the feeling of harmony between us were great. We curled up in front of the fire and laughed about our ridiculous situation.

"We have such a long and colourful history behind us. It will be good to see whether we can make it together now, without any major incidents," remarked Donald.

"I am looking forward to the future. Not long ago, I did not have a future. I hope you realise that you will have to be understanding towards me. I am getting stronger by the day, but I am not there yet. Though I am excited about being with you. As you once said, *'By your side and in your bed '.*"

"Before I forget, I need you to give me your passport and my engagement ring, if you still have it."

"Can I ask why?"

"I need the passport to apply for a Notice of Marriage Intention, and I am going to trade the engagement ring in for another – a bigger and better one. And this time I alone will choose it. I will also choose two wedding rings. I know you prefer platinum. You will not be disappointed. I have been told by my solicitor that my divorce could be finalised within six months, so I want us to be ready to marry."

"It all seems a little rushed, Donald—"

"You say that after all that you and I have been through? I am not wasting any time to put my affairs back in order. You had better think twice before you turn your back on me! This time I will not allow anything to go wrong! Do you understand me?" Donald hissed.

"OK. Please do not get angry. I just wondered about certain aspects of us marrying. For example, where will we be married, and where will we live after?"

"You are asking questions that you know the answers to. We will be married in the estate chapel, and we will live at Heatherfield Country Manor, as it should be. For pity's sake, Catherine, I am the squire and you will be my lady. Heatherfield Country Manor has always been the residence of the squire and his lady. Nothing is to change there." Donald was unquestionably irate.

There was quite a long silence between us.

"I presume Sheila and Jack will have left the manor. What about your mother and her partner, Peter? Will they have left? Please do not get angry with me. I would like some answers. Be careful, Donald – do not spoil things for us!" I spoke quietly, trying not to become emotional.

"You ask questions that have nothing to do with you. But if you want to know, fine! Sheila will receive a massive settlement from me. She has already made plans to move to Cheshire, where most of her family live. I am hoping that once things have settled down, I will have some sort of access to Jack. You will be the lady of Heatherfield Country Manor, and as such you have the authority to request that my mother and Peter leave. I will do my best to repair and decorate their cottage, so that they can return to their former home. Whether I can have that done in time, we will have to wait and see. I might call on my estate manager, Stuart Pennington, to help me. I don't know yet. I don't appreciate being questioned like this, Catherine. Don't make a habit of it!"

Too late. I was angry and emotional. "Is Sir Arthur still at the manor? Where is Bess? Are Jess and Jeremy still OK and at the manor? Is Babs still running the place? Who will be at our wedding? Will the priest marry us or a registry office person? Well? Don't you dare tell me that I am not in a position to ask you questions! I will ask as many questions as I need answers to. Do you understand?" I made a hasty retreat upstairs.

I ran a hot bath and lay in it for a long time. When I came out of the en-suite bathroom, Donald was lying on the bed, completely naked. He had made two hot coffees and poured two large whiskies. I laughed at him. He winked at me and beckoned me to lie by his side, which I did willingly.

His big hands caressed me. He kissed me and stroked my naked, wet body. I touched, licked, and kissed him. Slowly we played with each other. Soon we were having intercourse, slow, slow intercourse. There was no effort in loving Donald. I climaxed just before he did. We lay there, wrapped in each other's arms with a very damp sheet around us.

"Am I safe to talk to you now?" Donald laughed.

"Why? Have you something important to say to me?"

"Yes! Drink your coffee and have that whisky!"

We laughed. We threw the wet bedding off the bed and curled up under the duvet. Donald was asleep in no time.

I recalled Heatherfield Country Manor. The huge house was situated in a large estate. There was also an old castle on its grounds. I remembered seeing the place for the first time. Donald had taken me there to stay with him for quite a while. We approached through large wrought-iron gates and drove down a long drive to the pillared front door. All down the drive on both sides were different- coloured Scottish heathers: blue, white, purple, and rouge. The colours and scent were magnificent.

Standing in front of the manor, I was overwhelmed by the size of the place. Inside were numerous bedroom suites, tastefully decorated and dressed with beautiful bedding and curtains. From the huge entrance hall with its crystal chandeliers, doors led off into many rooms. There was cloakrooms, a large dining hall, a hall with a small stage for entertaining, a drawing room with large windows overlooking the gardens at the side of the manor, a large lounge with an inglenook fire, and a kitchen that had a large table and chairs in it. The manor also had its own library. It was truly impressive.

As I lay in bed now, I thought about Sir Arthur. When I lived at the manor with Donald, I had been so enthralled by a tapestry in the old castle that I decided to do some research about it. The tapestry hung in the entrance hall. It depicted a woman. Underneath her image were the words *From this day forth, you shall be known as Lady Catherine. I will love and protect you until the day I die.* The tapestry was hundreds of years old. That was where Donald got the idea to call me Lady Catherine, his love name for me. Once we were married, I would truly be The Much Honoured, Lady Catherine of the Thistle Isles.

Years ago, one night, when I was on my own in the manor, I sat by the fire with a supply of history books from the manor's library. I had already done some research online but had found nothing. I had had to unearth the books from storage. They had been preserved in archival boxes.

It seemed that during the thirteenth century, the English invaded Scotland, taking lands and property. The Scots fled. The English took over the McFadden castle, and Lady Catherine McFadden was held captive. A few years later the Scots re-took all their lands and the English retreated home. After this restoration, Lady Catherine was placed in a dungeon and only brought out when the squire had use of her. I presumed that she must had fallen in love with the English lord or knight.

As I sat by the large open fire in the lounge of the manor, I was aware that someone was standing in a corner of the room. I could see head armour with a nose protector, and a body vest made of knitted metal. The apparition disappeared as quickly as it had appeared. I was terrified!

I ran into the hallway, intending to lock myself in our bedroom. But the stairs in the hall were on the far side of the room and made of dark wood. It took forever to find them, frantic and disoriented as I was. I finally made it to our room and locked the door.

When Donald returned, he was so angry at me for reading the history books –and also for drinking so much whisky – that he forbade me from doing any more research. That was all well and good, but my apparition continued to appear at quite regular intervals. Sometimes he was in the lounge; other times he was on the stairs or in the hall. Every time I mentioned it to Donald, we argued. He told me not to mention it to anyone else.

I did learn that a Catholic priest had been summoned to conduct an exorcism a few years earlier, but in the end, he had only conducted a ceremony to bless the manor.

As time passed, my fear of the apparition faded. I called it Sir Arthur. I believed he had been an English lord or knight. I talked to him: "Good morning, Sir Arthur" or "Good evening, Sir Arthur". Donald laughed at me.

I wondered if Sir Arthur was still at the manor. Well, I would find out soon enough. On that note, I finally fell asleep.

Once we were up the following morning, we wasted no time driving to Scotland. The music was loud in the car. Donald drove fast. We laughed together, sang to the music together, and touched each other's hands now and again. We loved each other.

We arrived at the Thistle Resort just after lunch. As I walked over to the reception desk, I was greeted by Ruth, whom I had met before. I had previously phoned her and asked for one of the larger rooms, preferably with a balcony, as I was bringing a guest with me. The look on her face when Donald came in was a treat. "Good afternoon, Squire. Can I help you?" she said.

"The squire is my guest, Ruth," I said and took the key card.

Donald arranged for a porter to bring our luggage. Needless to say, the Squire Donald McFadden was a very important person in that region of Scotland. He was the laird of all the Thistle Islands. He was handsome, charming, and wealthy – and I had him all to myself.

Once in our beautiful room, we sat on the balcony and helped ourselves to a few drinks from the fridge bar. Unpacking was not on the agenda. Cuddles and a lovemaking session definitely were. We enjoyed the evening meal and, later, a few drinks in the bar with people we both knew. The whole day was magical.

We were only due to stay for a couple of days, but in fact we stayed for over a week. I busied myself with the resort's business. There was nothing hard or difficult about my duties. One or two days a month would be all they would require in future, but first I had to get used to the staff and the processes of running of the resort.

I spoke to Justin in America. He told me his wife and family were well and would love to see me again. He invited me to stay with them whenever I wanted to go. I told Justin about my relationship with Donald. He knew that history. It was his view that it had always been on the cards that Donald and I would get together once Thomas died.

I felt a little guilty that I had not given myself enough time to mourn the death of my husband. Donald, though, was such a force to deal with. He had always been so dynamic, and perhaps that was what I needed now.

My days were spent dealing with the resort and visiting with friends. Donald's days were spent managing his estate, meeting colleagues and friends, and riding over his grounds. He told me about visiting Sheila and his mother at the manor. He spent time with his baby son. He told them about our plans and was met with negativity from all concerned.

On the days that we had nothing to do, Donald took me sightseeing. We just loved our time together. Every night we enjoyed an evening meal, then drinks in the bar with friends. Afterwards was our intimate time in our beautiful room.

All too soon it was time for us to leave: Donald to his estate near Lancaster and I to my house. I made my goodbyes and told Ruth that I would return in about a month's time.

As we drove home, Donald turned the radio low. "I need to talk to you, Catherine. I have decided that I am not needed at the Lancastrian estate. I have a good stables' manager and a good estate manager. I am going to move back to my seat in Scotland. It is where I belong."

"Where does that leave me?" I asked quietly.

"That is up to you. I suggest that I find us a small cottage to rent on the Thistle estate. When you are ready, you can move there, and we will be together until such time as we can plan our marriage. You will be better placed for your employment at the Thistle Resort. You have more friends and acquaintances in Scotland than you do down south. I know you won't be as close to your sister and friends, but they can always come and visit you. What do you think?"

"Are you suggesting that I sell my house?"

"Well, it won't be of any use to you once we are settled in Scotland," he pointed out. "Anyway, it is just an idea for you to think about. I will be moving back to Scotland in the next few days. Open the glove compartment; there is something in there for you."

I opened the glove compartment. Inside was a leather ring case. I opened it to find the most beautiful engagement ring. A large single diamond was set on a broad platinum band. "Oh my goodness. Donald, it is magnificent."

"Put it on. It should fit, as it is the same size as the ring I traded in. I have insured it, but please be careful not to lose it. It fits next to the wedding ring that I have ordered!"

I was thrilled. I felt secure with Donald by my side.

Once back home, I wasted no time in visiting Margaret and all my friends to show them my beautiful engagement ring. My friends were happy for me, but Margaret was not. "You are walking right into the unhappiness that Donald is going to shower upon you. Mark my words, Catherine. Be very wary about Donald's intentions."

I was upset at the thought of Donald moving back to Scotland so soon after we became engaged. When he called on me just a few days later, I was shocked to learn he was packed and leaving that very minute. "I thought we could have a last night together," I lamented. "I was going to chill the wine and cook a meal. Then I would love you all night."

"Sorry, Catherine. At the moment I am not convinced that your heart is in the right place. You treat all this as if it is an elaborate game. I do not want to spend the night with you. There, I have said it. It shouldn't bother you much though." Donald jumped in his car and drove away.

I stood paralysed on my driveway. What the hell had happened there? Why was Donald so moody and upset? It was pointless phoning him; he would not answer his phone if he was driving. I decided to wait until the morning and phone him, seeking to understand why he was being so unreasonable.

The next morning, Donald actually phoned me bright and early. "I am sorry about yesterday. We should not have to be apart like this. Anyway, I have spoken to Stuart, my estate manager, and he tells me there are a couple of small cottages that we can choose between. Do you want me to go and look them over?"

"Of course I do. I do not want to live like this, with you up there and me down here. Do what you think is best for us. I am going to miss you, but I will be back at the hotel in three weeks. You might have settled on a cottage for us by then."

Three weeks soon went by. Just before I set off for Scotland, Donald phoned to tell me he had chosen a small, detached cottage in a village on his estate. "It is truly lovely and I know that you will adore it. It has front garden parking and a small rear garden. Two small bedrooms, but it will be big enough for you and me. I want you to see it before I make any decisions. Just to have you by my side and in my bed is all I care about."

I was excited and relieved. I had been wondering if Donald was having second thoughts about us. Now all I wanted to do was drive up to the Thistle Resort and hold and love Donald.

At last it was time for me to set off. TomTom the satnav was by my side, and it was a beautiful day. As I came off the motorways and dual carriageways, I found myself on country roads that passed through villages. I must admit, I was a little lost, but TomTom never let me down.

As I neared the Thistle Resort, I thought I saw Donald's car parked at a cottage. I turned my car round. Yes, it was Donald's car. The cottage looked beautiful and was situated in a picturesque village, so I presumed it was the cottage Donald had mentioned to me.

I parked at the side of the road and walked up to the front door. It was ajar, so I opened it fully and walked in. I was just about to shout a hello when I heard noises coming from up the stairs – the sounds of people having sex. There was no doubt about it. A man in particular was quite audible.

My blood ran cold. I knew before I even went to investigate that I was going to find Donald involved. But I had to see for myself.

I slowly went upstairs. I could see through the partly open bedroom door that Donald was on the bed with a woman, and they were both enjoying themselves, so much so that they did not notice me entering the bedroom.

Then, through the mirror of the dressing table, Donald caught sight of me. We looked into each other's reflected eyes. Donald looked away first and carried on with what he was doing. The woman didn't notice a thing.

I turned around, went back downstairs, and got into my car. I drove to the Thistle Resort, parked, and went straight to the room I had reserved.

I felt physically sick. What was I to do? I could not ignore what I had seen. Donald was so hard-faced, that he could well disregard that I had caught him in the act. It made me think perhaps Margaret had been right all those weeks ago when she said Donald might really want to get revenge.

I poured myself a drink from the room bar and sat on the balcony, waiting for something to happen. I suspected that Donald would show up and make out that it was all my fault. I decided I could not cope with heartache and upset; I would be better off without him. I had no intention of sitting by while he was unfaithful to me. I could not forgive him.

Reception phoned my room and said that Donald wished to see me in the hotel garden bar. He had not bothered to call my cell phone, as he knew that I would not have answered it. I put my make-up on and went to meet him.

"I have got you a drink " was his greeting. "A large whisky, as I think you need it. I need one too. I want you to hear me out. Please just listen. I am so very sorry that I had a quick fuck because it was on offer. I was weak, and it meant nothing to me. Please do not throw away what we have together because I acted like a stupid bastard. I hardly knew the woman. There was no affair. It was a one- off. There are no plans for me to run away with her. It was nothing."

"Do you want your ring back?" I asked sarcastically.

Donald looked angry. "You give me that ring back and I swear I will throw it into the lake. If you don't want it, neither do I. What are you going to do?"

"I believe that you are all about getting revenge on me. I have doubts that there was ever going to be a wedding. I think you were going to break my heart in some elaborate plan. So, I am going to call time on your plan and save my sanity."

"You are talking bloody rubbish. You are cold, Catherine. You are prepared to finish us without a second thought for me? And you will spite yourself just to get your own back and punish me? Have you forgot what you put me through not so long ago? You broke my heart and disrespected me. I gave us a second chance, but you are not prepared to do the same. All I wanted was for you to love me as much as you loved Hague. That is never going to happen, is it? Well, you are right. We are through. It was good while it lasted, and it went your way. Keep the ring and keep the memories. I don't want you."

And then Donald walked away. I heard his car drive away from the hotel car park.

I returned to my room and lay on the bed. I was still so jealous and upset. I fell asleep.

When I woke in the early hours of the morning, I knew that I had to contact Donald. I wanted to tell him that I loved him and did not want us to end it all. I tried phoning him, even though it was silly o'clock. He did not answer.

Over the following few days, I tried phoning him many times, but he still did not answer. I texted many, many times, but he never replied. I had to admit that things had gone too far and there would be no reconciliation.

I returned home and started to get my life back yet again.

C H A P T E R 5

Reconciliation

I continued with my normal routine. I visited my sister and went for meals with friends. I visited the golf club and resumed my duties on the committee. I booked a flight and went to Spain with Margaret and Matt. We stayed for two weeks.

Nothing seemed right. My thoughts were with Thomas. At least when Donald and I were together, I had not dwelt on depressing things. I had looked forward to my future with Donald. I had had a reason to get out of bed in a morning.

Five weeks after Donald left me in the hotel garden bar, I made a journey back to Scotland to fulfil my obligations to The Hague Corporation. I spent two days overseeing the administration of the Thistle Resort. When my duties were completed, I returned home. I did not see or hear from Donald, and I made no more effort to contact him.

Life carried on. Hilda, my housekeeper, became again a close friend. I went to Scotland every four weeks or so to honour my responsibilities.

On my last visit before the winter set in, Ruth, the resort manager, told me that she had seen Donald and he looked well. He had been accompanied by a very smart younger woman. "After I spoke to him, he left holding this woman's hand. They seemed extremely close."

"I don't suppose he asked about me?" I inquired.

Ruth laughed. "Catherine, what do you think? Especially as he was with someone else!"

Jealousy was deep in my body. I did not know how to handle it. I thought, *Well, you deserve to feel this way. You had choices, and as usual you made a selfish one. I miss him. I miss him holding me and making love to me. I wonder if he ever misses me in the same way?*

Just before I was due to set off for home, I took all the mail from reception and drove to the post office to hand it in over the counter. On the way back to the hotel to finish my packing, I found myself in the vicinity of Heatherfield Country Manor.

I could not resist it. I just wanted to see what the place looked like now. Had it changed since I lived there with Donald? Was Babs the housekeeper still there? There was only one way to find out.

I drove very slowly through the large entrance gates. As I reached the manor itself, I noticed that there were no cars parked there. I got out of my car and made my way round the rear of the building.

Babs was outside with the dogs. The dogs went berserk greeting me. Babs was pleased as well.

"I hope Donald and his mother aren't around," I said.

"No, everyone is out, so you can stop and have a coffee with me. It is so good to see you. What happened to you and Donald? I thought you were fine with each other. You should both know better after all this time. He is missing you, Catherine, and no doubt you are missing him as well."

"I very much doubt that he is missing me. He wants nothing more to do with me."

Just then, Donald burst into the kitchen. "What the fucking hell are you doing here?" he shouted.

"Hello to you too. Yes, I am fine. And you?" I said.

"I am taking the dogs for a walk. You had better be gone by the time I return. Who the hell do you think you are?" He collected the dogs and beat a quick retreat.

"Go on! Go on! Follow him! Walk with him!" urged Babs.

I hesitated, then took a deep breath and ran after him. "Wait, Donald. Wait. Please do not go so fast!"

I was surprised when he stopped and waited for me. "What do you want, Catherine?"

I looked into those beautiful blue eyes. My heart was beating loudly. The thrill of looking into his eyes made me say, "I have missed you! I am in love with you, Donald! I just wanted to see you again." I felt so defeated.

Donald walked away from me to make phone calls. He was busy for what seemed to be ages. Then he circled back and waited for me to join him. "What else do you want from me?" he asked.

"I want you to hold me. I want you to kiss me. I want us to start again. I have missed you more than you will ever know," I said.

"You must be joking! We cannot resume our relationship the way it was. There would have to be some changes."

"Anything you want. Just give me another chance!" I said, feeling very emotional.

The rain started in quite heavy. We were getting wet through. "I think I have the key to the chapel on this key ring," he said. "We can shelter there." We ran to the chapel in the distance, followed by the dogs. As luck had it, Donald did indeed have a key on his ring.

Donald lit some candles and placed them on the altar. It looked beautiful. I could not speak, I was so near to tears.

Just then the vestry door opened and in walked the priest, Father Benedict. "This is so unorthodox, Donald. Are you all right with this, Catherine?" he asked.

I was surprised to see the priest. When he asked me that question, I nodded. The rain on my face hid my tears.

As he put on his vestments, the priest said, "I have checked all the paperwork, and yes, it is still within the legal dates. Here are the rings that Babs gave me."

"Get on with it, Father!" snapped Donald.

Two of Donald's groundsmen walked in and stood at the back of the chapel. "Here are our two witnesses," said Donald.

"Read the vows from this card," the priest instructed him.

"In the name of God, I, Donald James McFadden, take you, Catherine Hague, to be my wife, to have and to hold from this day forward, for better or worse, for richer or poorer, in sickness and in health and to love, be faithful, and cherish all the days of my life. From this day forth you shall be known as Lady Catherine McFadden. I shall love and protect you for the rest of my life. This is my solemn vow."

The priest then gave me the card and asked me to read the vows. I was desperately trying to hold everything together. It was such an emotional time, and the last thing I wanted to do was to blub my words out.

"In the name of God, I, Catherine Hague, take you, Donald James McFadden, to be my husband, to have and to hold from this day forward, for better or worse, for richer or poorer, in sickness and in health, and to love, be faithful and cherish all the days of my life. This is my solemn vow."

"You may now exchange rings. Donald, place the ring on Catherine's finger. Catherine, place the ring on Donald's finger. What God has brought together, let no man separate. I now pronounce you man and wife. You may kiss."

I looked at Donald and he looked back at me. We kissed and kissed.

"I wish you all to sign this register, and then you may go. Congratulations, Donald and Catherine!"

After signing the register, we collected our marriage certificate. Donald gave the groundsmen some money and told them to have the day off. He warned them not to tell anyone about it until after six o'clock, as he had to tell his mother first.

We walked out of that chapel as man and wife. We looked like drowned rats. Donald was laughing and hugging and kissing me. We were ecstatic.

I asked him how on earth he had managed to arrange our wedding. He told me that when he realised I wanted to come back to him, he telephoned Father Benedict and told him to collect the wedding rings from Babs. "Simple! Did you notice that I added the line from the tapestry?"

"Yes, I did, and it was lovely," I replied.

"I really love you so much, Catherine, I promise to love you forever, and I promise to be faithful. I will never let you down. All I want to do is to make you happy. If you are happy, I also shall be happy."

"I am so much in love with you. I have missed you so much. I also promise to love and be faithful. I intend to make you a very happy man!"

The rain kept pouring down on us. Donald's phone rang. With a heavy sigh, he told me he was needed at the stables. The vet had arrived, and it looked as if a prize mare was going to lose the twin foals she was expecting. He had no choice but to go to her.

I understood. The priest gave Donald a lift to the stables, and I walked back to the manor in the rain with the dogs. I put the dogs in the outside kennel. I made my way into the kitchen, where I was met by Babs. I showed her my finger with the wedding ring on, and she burst into floods of tears.

Mrs McFadden, Donald's mother, slammed into the kitchen. She aimed a barrage of abuse at me. At one point, I thought that she was going to spit at me. Babs tried to intervene. "Wait, Madam. Please listen!"

"No, Babs," I said. It was not our duty to tell his mother about our marriage. I preferred to leave that to Donald.

"Get out of this house and off my property. Don't you ever set foot in this house again! How dare you! You have done nothing but bring trouble and heartache to this family. You are a low-life gold digger who thinks herself above her station. It is because of you that Donald cannot see his only son. Leave now or I will personally throw you out. Mark my words, Donald will hear about this, and perhaps he will see you for what you are!"

"Don't worry, Mrs McFadden. I am leaving."

As I walked out to my car, she slammed the door on me. I waited a few moments, then rushed back to the kitchen and gave Babs my card. "Phone me later," I said and made my retreat.

I drove back to the hotel and sat outside, overlooking the lake. I was absolutely wet through, so sitting in the rain for a little more time made no difference. I was thrilled that Donald had arranged our wedding. When I woke up that morning, I had been missing Donald, and now at mid-afternoon, I was Donald's wife.

I thought, Right. *I need to shower, dry my hair, and dress myself in my best clothes. I must look my very best when Donald comes – whenever that may be!*

As I entered the reception area, Ruth came over and said that some flowers had been delivered. She thought they should have been delivered to the manor. The flowers were addressed to Mrs McFadden, and the message on the card read: *From the person who loves you the most – Your Husband.*

"Those flowers are for me," I said. I showed Ruth my wedding ring.

She was shocked. "When did this happen? Never mind. You need to go to your room now. Once word gets out, journalists will descend upon us. Go. I will arrange for the flowers to be taken to your room. Shall I bring you something to eat or drink?"

"No, thank you. I am going to shower and rest up."

I did ask her to find me the phone number of the estate's office. After my shower, I phoned through to Mr Stuart Pennington, the estate manager. I introduced myself and asked for his help. I told him that, by way of a wedding present for my husband, the squire, I wished him to find and purchase two toy-sized pot-bellied pigs. Donald had always wanted pigs.

"Sorry, Lady McFadden, but surely that is for the farm manager to sort out? When did you and the squire marry? Anyway, I am far too busy at the moment, so I will give you the farm manager's phone number."

"I thought you were in full control of the estate, including the farm section? I suggest you phone the farm manager on my behalf. I too am very busy. When arranged, send the bill to me, care of the Thistle Resort. Do you understand?"

There was no reply. I presumed that Mr Pennington had cut me off. What a disagreeable man!

That night, I ate a meal in my room. Donald phoned me a few times just to talk. We were both elated. But he had yet to speak to his mother.

I spent some time phoning all the people whom I wished to know about my marriage. Margaret congratulated me, but I could tell she had her reservations. I spoke to my daughters, but I did not know where my son was. Nothing new there. I even phoned Justin, who was pleased for us. He said I should bring Donald to America with me for a holiday.

Life had to go on, but now and again Thomas crept into my head and my soul. I would have given anything to see him one more time. How selfish was that?

Ten o'clock came, and Donald arrived from the manor. He had eaten, washed and changed. When I asked him about his mother and her reaction to our news, he would not discuss it. "Nothing to report," he said. "Come here, Catherine. I just want to hold and love you. I am very tired, but it is our wedding night, so … take those bloody clothes off and lie on the bed with me!"

I did as Donald asked. As I lay on the bed, Donald removed his clothes. We were both laughing about the clinical situation. We kissed and held each other for a short while.

"Lie on your front," requested Donald, and I did so. He stroked my back right down to between my legs. He opened my legs and then lay on top of me, his hands underneath me, holding and squeezing my breasts. His grip grew tighter and tighter. I could feel his penis between my legs, and then I felt his penetration inti my vagina.

He was not gentle – he was quite rough, but he did not hurt me. He kissed, sucked, and bit the nape of my neck. He was quite carried away. When he whispered, "Come on, Catherine! Come on, Catherine!" I had a most powerful orgasm. I felt Donald ejaculate. We lay still for quite a while.

As Donald drifted into sleep, I had to ask him to move – I was trapped under him and could not get out. When he moved for me, I cuddled him. We fell asleep in each other's arms.

CHAPTER 6

Married

The next morning, we woke together to the sun shining and the birds singing. We knew that we had the rest of our lives together, to enjoy and experience all that the world could offer.

A champagne breakfast was delivered to our room, courtesy of the Thistle Resort. We both enjoyed it, and when we had finished, Donald said, "Go and pack your things. We will move to the manor now!"

"You know how I feel about that. I will not live there with your mother and Peter. I will not change my mind, Donald, so don't waste your breath!"

"I have the builders working on my mother's cottage, but it will take a further eight weeks before it will be ready for them. Am I to flit between the manor and this hotel room, not forgetting that in a few weeks' time it will be Christmas and Hogmanay? What is to happen then?"

"I will attend all the festive occasions, but I will not sleep at the manor until your mother has left for good."

Donald looked at a loss.

"Listen, Donald, I am looking forward to us cuddling up in the lounge, in front of the fire, and perhaps having good sex there like we used to do. How can we live like that with your mother and Peter around? At least here in this room we have all the privacy I need to make you a very happy man!" I kissed his neck and face.

Donald agreed that perhaps he should be patient. I told him that, while

I would not be there, I was going to refurbish the large front bedroom for us to have when I moved in. "You can keep your room as a man cave, but you and I will have a large queen bed in the front bedroom as our marital bed. And by God, am I looking forward to us being together between those sheets."

Donald smiled and nodded.

It was inevitable that he had to go to the stables to check on the mare. He phoned me from there to say that it looked as if the foals were still all right inside their mum. The vet would keep visiting her, and the staff would take good care of her.

"When you are ready, meet me at the stables," he instructed. "I have found your riding gear – that is, I think it is your riding gear as it was in the back of my wardrobe. I don't think I've had another woman staying with me who brought her own gear. but I could be mistaken …"

"Be careful, husband! Be very, very careful!"

We laughed.

The days that followed were marvellous. Donald continued to work at the stables, and I continued to work at the Thistle Resort. Donald would meet his mates after work and go for a drink in the little local pubs. We would meet up at the hotel for a good evening meal, and then retire to our lovely room, where we cuddled and had sex. Donald had no problem satisfying me and I had no trouble satisfying him. Every night we slept wrapped around each other.

One day Babs phoned me to tell me that Donald's mother and Peter were to go away for a few days. I made arrangements to arrive at the manor when they were not there. I took Babs upstairs to tell her what I wanted doing to the front bedroom.

The front bedroom was dark. I wanted a builder to convert one of the large windows to a French window with a Juliet balcony. Decorators would paint the whole room white. The floor had to be left as it was; the original wood boards were still intact.

The curtains would be long and dark-green velvet. I didn't mind about the bedding, as long as it was dark green and sky blue. Woollen rugs would surround the queen bed. To decorate the walls, I would choose among the paintings in the manor.

While I had a decorator, I wanted him to paint another of the bedrooms sky blue. Perhaps Donald would make this into a nursery for baby Jack. The room adjacent would make a fine bedsit for a nanny, but that job, I thought, was best left for a later date, when I had Donald's permission.

All I had to do was contact Mr Stuart Pennington again and ask him to supply me with an approved builder's contact details.

As I expected, Mr Pennington was far from helpful. He insisted that he had more than enough work for the estate's preferred builder, and he could not spare him at the moment. He was not prepared to take the builder off an important job for me to use on something frivolous. The cheek of him!

Just in time, Donald phoned me to say that he was thrilled with the two pigs. He named one Butch and the other Spoilt. He said he was Butch and I was Spoilt, and he thought that was hilarious. "On your bike!" I said. We laughed.

I took the opportunity to tell him that Stuart Pennington was unhelpful. What did he suggest I do? Donald insisted that Pennington had the run of the whole estate, and that he could not interfere. "You can try appealing to his better nature, but I don't think he has one!"

Babs had a relative who was a qualified decorator, so that was good. I trusted Babs to oversee the job, and she could arrange for all of the soft furnishings.

That night I asked Donald what Stuart Pennington was really like. I knew I would have to see him if I was ever going to persuade him to let me have the builder for a day or so.

"Stuart is gay and lives with his partner, I think he is called Jonathan. They have been together for quite a few years. He is in his late forties as we are. In fact, I used to go to school with him. My, that was a long time ago!" said Donald.

The next day, I drove to the estate offices. The car park was full, so I parked by the roadside. I entered the building and the receptionist took me into Stuart's office.

The first person I saw was a woman – the same woman who had been fucking Donald when I caught them in the act. I was somewhat taken aback. I looked towards Stuart's desk. He raised his head from his computer, and our eyes met.

I went into shock. He had the same eyes as Thomas – deep, dark eyes. I thought I was looking directly into Thomas's eyes.

I stuttered some excuse and ran to my car. By the time I had sat in the driver's seat, I was crying uncontrollably.

The passenger door opened and Stuart entered. "I presume you recognised Linda and that is why you are crying."

"Don't be so ridiculous!" I snapped, trying to stop myself from crying. "I do not care about seeing that woman. Why should I?"

"Then why are you so upset?"

I composed myself and apologised for my outburst. "Please do not mention this to Donald," I said.

Stuart's eyes looking deep into mine sent sexual thrills all over me. He put his arm around me, I assume to comfort me. I enjoyed the physical contact. He felt like Thomas used to feel. Their features were not alike, but he had dark skin, dark eyes, and dark hair. He was physically built like Thomas and he smelt like Thomas. My imagination was working overtime!

"I am so sorry and embarrassed, Mr Pennington. I am all right now," I whispered.

"Stuart, please. I would like an explanation though. I will understand if it is because of Lin—"

"No," I interrupted. "It has nothing to do with that woman!"

"Fine! If you are sure you are all right, I bid you good day." Stuart got out of the car and went back into his office. I wasted no time in driving back to the hotel and retreating to the privacy of my room.

I lay on the bed, trying to make sense of what had happened. I could still recall Stuart's eyes and the feel of him holding me. I felt the comfort. I recalled the sexual attraction.

It was his eyes that had started a chain reaction. He reminded me so much of my dead husband that I was confusing memories with reality. Oh, what must Stuart Pennington think of me? A blubbering, stupid woman!

How could I put this right? I knew I would have to see him again, not only to get the builder but to tell him the truth about Thomas. I would not show myself up again. Or so I thought.

That night, when Donald had been watered and fed, he settled down to read and listen to music. "What have you done today?" he asked.

"Believe it or not, I went to see the superior Mr Pennington. Though I didn't have much luck in finding the details for a builder, I met his assistant Linda. Do you know this Linda?"

Donald looked up from his reading. Glaring over his glasses, he said, "Don't play me, Catherine. I will not rise to your games. Do you understand me?" He seemed very angry.

At least that answered my questions. It was obvious he knew her quite well.

Donald wanted to know what was going to happen to us over the Christmas and Hogmanay period. I explained that I had made arrangements earlier to spend Christmas with my daughters and grandchildren. That would leave Donald to have Christmas with his family at the manor. If he wanted, he could see his son on Christmas Day.

As far as Hogmanay was concerned, I expected to be at the castle to celebrate it with Donald. "I would like to have a room at the castle. I will be civil to your mother, but obviously she will return to the manor that night."

Donald explained that there were no other clans to coordinate with for the celebrations this year, so invitations had gone out only to a few friends and the staff. He had ordered me a McFadden tartan scarf to go over my shoulders and fasten at the side of my dress. All I had to do was find a plain dress that would match the tartan. No pressure there, then!

The following week, I returned to the estate office. Stuart was not at his desk. I asked Linda if he was available. She told me that he was in a meeting but probably would not be that long. I told her that I would wait in my car if she would be good enough to tell him that I wished to see him. I returned to my car and nervously sat waiting.

Soon, Stuart was getting in the passenger side. "What now, Catherine?"

"I have come to apologise for my unacceptable behaviour and also to give you an explanation."

"I do not need an explanation. I am really busy—"

"Please just give me a few minutes."

Stuart just sat there in silence, so I continued, "Not long ago, I lost my husband Thomas. He went away and he is not coming back." I stopped to compose myself. "I have found it really hard to deal with. I am on a roller coaster that is taking me down and down, and I cannot get off it. Donald has been most supportive. I have tried counselling and all the other things, and I thought that I was slowly coming to terms with my loss."

Again I stopped to compose myself. "On my first visit here, when you looked up, I felt I was looking into Thomas's eyes. For a few moments, I was transported to a different time, a different place. Memories flooded back. I have never cried over his death, but the other day I just was so emotional that I burst into tears. You look nothing like Thomas, but you have his eyes and … and you smell so familiar." I stopped.

Stuart placed his arms around me, and there was no way I could hold back my tears. "Come, Catherine, stop crying!

I am not your Thomas, am I? I do understand where you are coming from. I lost someone I loved dearly quite a long time ago, and it does not seem to get any easier.

"I shall tell you what I used to do. I used to find a cupboard. That is, a place, any place where I could not be found, where I could not be interrupted. In that cupboard, I would cry. I would cry and cry until I could no longer cry. I then resumed my normal duties. I thought that this helped me. I don't know if it would help you, but you could give it a try."

I looked up into his beautiful eyes. I felt the sexual chemistry raging through me, and I also knew that Stuart Pennington was aware of it. He took his arms away from me. I said, "No, hold me for a little longer. Kiss me, please!"

"No way, Catherine. You have to get a grip. I am Stuart Pennington and not Thomas. Please do not bring your problems to me. I don't think I can help you. Donald should get you more counselling."

"Please, please do not tell Donald about this, I beg of you! I will not bother you again – *after* you have agreed to help me with a builder." We laughed and shook hands.

A few days later, Donald had to arrange delivery of a mare to Ireland. He said he thought it best if he went as well. I had no objection, but I knew that I would miss him. He would be away for four days.

I kissed him goodbye that morning, and I knew that he was going to miss me as well. Obviously, the honeymoon period had not ended for either of us.

Justin called to tell me that Virgin Airlines had a really good offer on a one-way ticket to LA. It was an open ticket, so he suggested that I buy it and keep it until I wanted to fly over. He added that Thomas's final resting place had been finished, and offered to buy my return ticket when the time came. I did just as he suggested.

Later that morning, as I was in my office, one of the girls from reception came in and said, "There is a Mrs McFadden asking to see you, Lady Catherine. She is waiting in reception."

I felt quite uneasy at this news, but I instructed the girl to take Mrs McFadden into a small, quiet lounge. When I walked into this room, Mrs McFadden stood up and straight away said, "Hello, Catherine. I am not here to cause any trouble. All I ask is that you are civil with me and listen to what I have to say."

I nodded and asked if she would like a coffee or tea. To my surprise, she asked if she could have a coffee. I ordered coffee for us and sat down.

"All that time ago, when we were arranging a wedding for Sheila and Donald, we were aware that it was you Donald wanted to be with. Please understand that as Donald's mother, I wanted what was best for him. I believed he should marry and have children. In a way, you did him a favour by not going through with the marriage. Donald was hurt and upset, but he did agree to marry Sheila and they were blessed with Jack.

"Still, I knew that they were not happy. I was not surprised when I found out that Donald was to divorce Sheila and marry you. You are now Lady Catherine McFadden, and as such I want you to come and live at the manor. Peter and I are looking forward to moving back into our cottage, but it is going to be a few more weeks yet. With Christmas and New Year coming upon us, I really would like you to be living with us all at the manor. It would give you and me time to put disagreements behind us. What do you say?"

"I appreciate what you are saying, Mrs McFadden. Unfortunately, I have plans to spend Christmas with my daughters and grandchildren. It was arranged a long time ago, and I do not want to cancel. I will be at the castle on New Year's Eve with you and the family, but please understand that I really want to start my new life at the manor when it is just Donald and me. No disrespect to you. I have a lovely suite here where Donald and I are most comfortable."

"That is fine. If you change your mind, you are very welcome to move in. I hope that perhaps you will forget our unpleasant disagreements."

I nodded and shook Mrs McFadden's hand as she left.

The week before Christmas came up fast. I bought presents for my family and friends back home. I had not seen any of them for quite some time, although we kept in constant touch.

While shopping in the city, I was pleased to buy an evening dress that would be perfect for New Year's Eve. It was in a lovely shade of blue that would complement the McFadden tartan. I bought Donald a beautiful tie pin that could also be worn with his full Scottish outfit. I purchased many small gifts for people like Babs and Ruth.

I was glad when I finished with Christmas shopping. I was not a great fan of Christmas, or of the New Year for that matter. In fact, I was a boring person. I enjoyed quiet home comforts, though, at the moment I had no home comforts as such.

A few days before Christmas, I said my goodbyes to Donald and drove carefully to my daughter Carol's home. Carol had also invited my younger daughter Jennifer for Christmas.

The grandchildren were growing up so quickly. My son- in-law, Jim, made me feel welcome. None of us had any idea where my son Tony was, but he did phone us now and again. He seemed very happy and contented.

I told them of my situation: the fact that I was living in the Thistle Resort but soon would be moving into the manor. I invited them all to come and visit Donald and me.

On Christmas Eve, I phoned Donald. To my surprise, he was at the estate's Christmas party. Of course he was! Why had I not thought there would be such a thing as the estate's Christmas party? I had been so wrapped up in my own Christmas itinerary that I honestly had not thought about Donald and what he was going to do.

He sounded quite drunk. In the background, I heard someone calling to him. It was a woman's voice and she was shouting, "Hurry up! I'm waiting to dance."

"Who was that?" I asked Donald.

"Who was what?"

"Was someone asking you to dance? I don't suppose it was Linda, was it?"

"You are doing it again, Catherine. I have told you before – do not play me! Does it matter who I dance with? You chose not to be with me over Christmas, so to hell with you. I might even take her home. What do you say to that, eh? Go and enjoy yourself, because I intend to do!"

He hung up. I called back. His phone was turned off. I left several messages to let him know that I was missing him.

I tried phoning him several more times that night, but his phone remained switched off. Then I became so angry that I did not try him again.

Christmas Day was magical. After church, we went back to Jim and Carol's. We opened all our presents. The grandchildren were, like any other children on Christmas Day, very excited. They busied themselves with new clothes and toys.

Around lunchtime, I phoned Donald to wish him merry Christmas. He was very quiet. I told him that I was really missing him, but I got no response from him. "Have you been to see Jack?" I asked.

"No, why should I?"

"Because it is Christmas?" I sarcastically replied. "Do you not want to go and see him? Have you bought him a Christmas present?"

"No and no. Mother has tried to make arrangements to visit him and to take him some presents, but Sheila is having none of it."

"Donald, is all this because of me? If it is, I will personally go and see Sheila when I get back."

"Don't flatter yourself. This is nothing to do with you. It is family business!"

I was angry and upset. "Don't you ever say that to me! I am your wife, and therefore I am your closest family – or I should be! Do you know what? I don't want to talk to you. I was missing you, and you have just ruined my day. To hell with you, Donald!"

Afterwards I was so fretful that I took myself for a long walk. Thomas had never upset me intentionally, but Donald could be so cruel. I knew that I should never compare the two, but I still felt such a closeness to Thomas.

We all enjoyed the Christmas dinner but I told them I would feel happier if I went back to Donald on Boxing Day. There were no objections. Again I promised that once I moved into the manor, I wanted them to come and stay with us for a good family holiday. I told the grandchildren that I would take them pony riding, and they were thrilled.

The following day, I said my goodbyes and drove back to Scotland. I went straight to my hotel room to unpack and freshen up. I tried phoning Donald, but his phone was switched off again.

All dressed up and looking good, I made some enquiries at our reception desk as to where Donald was likely to be on a Boxing Day evening. Armed with the name of the venue, I made my way to a local inn.

I walked into the long bar, and straight away I noticed Donald standing there with that Linda on a bar stool by his side. I just stood waiting for Donald to turn around and see me, which he did. He rushed over, and we kissed and kissed and kissed some more. I heard someone ask who was I. Someone else replied, "His wife."

"I have missed you so much!" whispered Donald. "Don't you ever leave me again! All I wanted to do was sit by a fire with you in my arms. I have been so lonely without you!"

"Then I suggest we go back to our room and cuddle up all night," I whispered back.

We made a hasty retreat. To hell with Linda. I was the one Donald wanted to be with, to love and cuddle up with, and that would do for me. Back at the hotel, we hit the room bar and loved each other all night.

I did not mention his son Jack. I did not want any more trouble. But I was determined that one day I would go to see Sheila and find out why she would not let Donald see his own son. I wanted to find out if it was because of me. I was sure that I could help to resolve that nasty situation.

The celebration of Hogmanay was upon us. Donald changed into his Scottish garb at the manor, while I booked into our room for the night and spent the afternoon there, getting ready for the ball.

The evening entertainment included a five-course dinner, followed by bands, pipers, dancing, and fireworks. I was looking forward to it all. I promised Donald that I would be civil to his mother and Peter her partner.

I was very pleased with the look of my evening dress with the McFadden tartan draped over it. As usual, Donald looked handsome in his kilt. The majority of the men were in traditional attire. Donald, his mother, Peter, other McFaddens, and I were seated at the top table.

Donald walked around with me, introducing me to many, many people. It was great being there with our friends like William and Ann. The food and entertainment were superb. After the meal, Donald resumed his tour of all the tables, introducing me to anyone who had not met me.

"Catherine, come here. I believe this is one person you were eager to meet," said Donald as he stood in front of a tall, handsome, middle-aged man.

"Sorry?" I said to him. I had no idea who he was.

"Jonathan," he said, solving the mystery. "How do you do, Catherine? Stuart has told me all about you."

I was bewildered. He was so good-looking. I began to panic as Jonathan's words sank in. I wondered if Stuart really had told him everything.

Just then Stuart came up beside me and said that he was pleased that at last I had met his partner Jonathan. Stuart made our excuses to Jonathan, and we walked onto the dance floor. "What is the matter, Catherine?" asked Stuart as he held me close. I could feel thrills racing through my body.

"Please tell me that you have not said anything to Jonathan about me and … things?" I whispered.

"I swore to you that nobody would ever be told about you and I. I am not in the habit of breaking my word!"

"I love the way you make me feel."

"Stop it, Catherine – although I will admit that at this moment you feel fucking good." Stuart laughed.

"Stuart Pennington, you are letting your guard down!" I laughed back at him.

When the music stopped, I returned to the top table and to Donald. That was the last I saw of Stuart and his partner until just after midnight. While we were all in the courtyard watching the fireworks, Stuart came up to me and wished me happy New Year. He kissed me on the lips for just a couple of seconds, long enough to confirm that we were strongly sexually attracted to each other. I did not see him again that night.

When I was in the ladies' restroom, Ann, the wife of Donald's best friend William, came over to talk to me. She invited me to a ladies' coffee morning and table sale in the New Year. I accepted, pleased to have been invited.

"You know, it is uncanny how much you resemble Donald's first wife, Christine," said Ann.

"What happened to her? I have heard a few stories, but I never really liked to pry."

"They were very young. Donald was besotted with her. There was a nasty accident. While they were out riding together, Christine took a bad fall. She died before the medics got to her. Please do not tell Donald that we have been talking like this. He has never mentioned Christine since that accident."

"No, of course not. I was just being curious. I am wife number three now," I said, and we giggled together.

The night was a fantastic success. Donald and I retired to our bedroom in the hotel part of the castle. As usual, we cuddled up together, and then Donald made an announcement. "Mother and Peter are moving out of the manor in two weeks' time. So, my beautiful Catherine, you shall be coming home with me then. I am not going to waste any more time. When Mother moves out, you move in, and then the real fun begins!"

I laughed at his excited attitude. But I must admit, I also was excited at the prospect of moving into the manor as Donald's wife, Lady Catherine McFadden.

CHAPTER 7

The Manor

A couple of weeks after Hogmanay, Donald came to our room at the hotel, washed, and dressed for an evening meal with me. Some nights we just had dinner together. Other nights we would have dinner, and Donald would stop the night with me. On those occasions, he would disappear in the early hours to resume his duties at his stables.

That particular night, Donald was all excited. "Guess!"

"I have no idea what you wish me to guess!"

"On Wednesday afternoon, about two o clock, I shall be collecting you from here and taking you home! Pack all your belongings on Tuesday, and they will be sent to the manor. On Wednesday, all I will have to do is collect my wife and take her directly home. What do you think of that?"

"Wow. I really don't know what to say. Have your mother and Peter moved into their cottage?"

"Yes, and even my mother was thrilled by the changeover and chaos. I can't wait. I am so looking forward to you and me living together. Remember, you promised you would be 'by my side and in my bed,'" remarked Donald. "You can now arrange to sell your house. You have no more need of it."

Wednesday came soon enough. That afternoon, I waited down in reception for Donald to come and collect me. Memories came flooding back of waiting in a hotel reception for Thomas Hague. He walked in to meet me, so tall, handsome, and sexy. I recalled that night. We had sex, and I knew that I would love Thomas Hague forever and a day.

I still loved him with such passion, but he was no longer here. Donald McFadden was. Strange that I could not cry at losing Thomas, but as soon as I saw Stuart Pennington, my emotions flooded out as tears.

Donald arrived, all dressed up, in his large white Mercedes. He looked vibrant and alive. I felt very proud to be his wife. "Come on, Lady Catherine McFadden!" he shouted. "Your carriage awaits."

I left my car up in the hotel car park, ready for me to collect at a later date.

As we drove up the long drive to the manor. I could see all the budding heathers. At the entrance to the Manor there was a small welcoming party: Babs, the housekeeper, the chamber girl, the groundsmen, and of course my two babies – Jess and Jeremy, the golden retrievers. I greeted them with all the excitement I felt. Donald then lifted me high and carried me over the threshold. I felt embarrassed.

As I walked into the kitchen with Babs, she said, "The welcome reception will be at seven o'clock. You and Donald will make your entrance into the large dining hall at about twenty past seven."

"Whoa! What reception, Babs?" I asked.

"Has Donald not mentioned it to you?"

"No, Donald has not mentioned it to me. Perhaps it is not a welcome reception for me but for someone else!"

Donald came then and picked me up again. Without saying anything, he carried me upstairs and put me down in the newly revamped front bedroom. It was gorgeous. Babs had really done me proud.

"When were you going to mention the reception tonight, husband dear?" I asked.

"After I made love to you, cuddled you, had sex with you, kissed you all over, and had sex with you again. I did not want you to be distracted!" Donald laughed.

He was so eager, I had no time to undress. He undressed me and himself. As usual, we were so aroused that it was not long before we were between the sheets, enjoying each other.

After we made love, my thoughts drifted off again to the time when I was with Thomas Hague. I knew it was wrong to have another man on my mind at that moment, but I enjoyed the feeling I received when I thought about Thomas.

Donald held me close and said, "We shall have a wonderful life together, you and I. We are so alike. We bounce off each other in all aspects. I love you so much. I will never let you down. Not intentionally, anyway. I have too much to lose if I ever hurt you. I hope you feel the same way too. I know you do not love me as much as you loved Thomas Hague, but one day you will. Watch this space!"

I did not know what to say. I found it very hard to talk about my love for Thomas. "Donald, you know that I love you. I promise that I will make you a very happy man," I replied. "Now, I have to shower and start preparing for tonight."

"Good idea. I will shower with you. No objections, wife – you do as I say!" Donald said, laughing as he pulled me towards the shower.

Smart casual was the dress code for the reception, but Donald wanted me to wear something more like an evening dress with all the make-up and jewellery. He chose my dress and chose well.

"Who is coming tonight?" I asked.

"At least thirty people, most of whom you know. I cannot remember the full invitation list, but there will be Mother and Peter, Babs and her husband, our priest, the stable manager and his wife, the farm manager and his wife, Ruth and her guest, William and Ann, a few other friends of ours, the headmistress of our primary school, the head of our Women's Institute and so on. In fact, anyone you will have dealings with as lady of the manor will be there."

Why was Stuart not mentioned? I had to ask. "What about the estate manager and his partner?"

"No, they were unable to come, but I am instructed to wish you all the best from Stuart. He said he was sorry not to be able to be with us tonight, but he wishes you all the best in your new home and position."

I really wanted to know why Stuart could not come, but I thought it inappropriate to ask that straight out.

At seven twenty, Donald escorted me into the large dining hall. Everyone was seated around a huge dining table. They stood and I was introduced. In the past, the dining hall had been used for grand balls and gatherings of the estate. It was very old. The dark wood panels made the whole place look depressive. The room was very well lit on this occasion, however. The food was delicious and the company was more than entertaining. Jokes were told, and the guests laughed.

Before dessert, I excused myself to go to the cloakroom to freshen up. As I walked across the entrance hall, there he was, in a corner. I kept my eyes on Sir Arthur. I did not want him to disappear. He looked as he had always looked: a shadowy outline of a soldier dressed in dark clothes, a head helmet that had a nose protector, and a tunic vest that looked like woven steel. I could easily make out the soldier's armour.

I was not afraid. I had seen him so many times now. In a way, I was pleased that he had returned to see me. Nobody else currently living at the manor had ever reported any sightings.

As the apparition melted away, I called after it, "Thank you for coming to see me, Sir Arthur."

I knew I must never speak of Sir Arthur to Donald – or anybody else, for that matter. Donald used to get so angry about it.

When all the guests had gone, Donald started to laugh about all the duties I had been asked to perform as the wife of the squire. He had overheard all my conversations. I had been asked to join the board of the school's governors, the Women's Institute wanted to have the use of the large hall for their annual charity ball, the primary school invited me on regular visits to meet the children, and so on and so forth. "At this rate, I will need my own PA if I am to complete all these duties and work at the Thistle Resort," I said. Oh, how Donald laughed!

At last we were cuddled up in a warm bed. It was our first night together in my beautiful room. Donald was nearly asleep, but I wanted to talk to him. "I know that we are very contented in each other's company. Now that I am in your bed as your wife, I need to know that I can talk to you about anything."

"Go to sleep, Catherine. We will talk tomorrow."

"But I need to mention something to you now, and I do not want you to get angry with me."

"I will never get angry with you. I will always support you. What is all this about?"

"I saw Sir Arthur tonight. He was in the hallway when I went to the cloakroom."

"Not this again! I have told you that it is your imagination. You must stop this nonsense. If you are afraid, then you must do something to get over it! I told you last time you were living here that you must not mention this. You will be called the madwoman at the manor! Now go to sleep and don't mention it again!"

"Do you know, it is *so* reassuring to know that I can ask you anything and you will always support me."

Donald whispered in my ear, "Fuck off, Catherine!" We laughed and kissed each other.

I really wanted to talk about our role in the life of his son Jack, but that night was clearly not the right time to bring the subject up.

The following day was special. Donald was to stay with me all day. After a hearty breakfast, we walked through all the garden areas. I took Donald to an old stone shelter and tried to explain what I wanted to do with it. As far as Donald was concerned, I could do anything I wanted within reason. I offered to pay the costs, as I knew that the estate manager would not give me the help I needed if he thought it was going to be too expensive.

We discussed our honeymoon. Because Donald did not want a beach resort, I suggested Malta. I had been to Malta many times, and I knew he would love the place. A good hotel and a hire car, and we could sightsee to our heart's content.

Then I took a deep breath and started a conversation about the baby. "Jack is two in March, is he not?"

"Yes, he is."

"Are we going to have any role in his life? Do you not want him to come and stay here now and again?"

"Stop this now, Catherine. Jack has nothing to do with you. You and I are all right as we are. I do not want our relationship and life to be disturbed by a small child. Please leave everything as it is!"

"Right! Stop shouting at me! I am not one of your clucking hens. I am your wife, and as such I deserve an explanation as to what is going to happen with Jack. I honestly believe that it is because of me that Sheila won't let you or anyone in your family see the baby. Am I right?"

"If that is all that is bothering you, put your mind at rest. It is nothing to do with you. Are you OK now?"

I did not answer him. I was still convinced that it was because of me that Donald was missing out on Jack 's early years, but I had to respect Donald's wishes.

A few weeks went by. I was so happy. A few times I stopped and thought about Thomas, but it seemed to be getting easier to control my pain and anger.

Stuart Pennington was also in my thoughts. He was the only person who had an emotional hold over me as strong as Thomas's. I only had to look into his beautiful dark eyes, and memories of Thomas came flooding back.

I enjoyed walking the dogs around the gardens early in the morning. I loved to stop by the old stone shelter. If it was cold or rainy, I huddled there with the dogs.

One particularly nasty morning, I was in the shelter when I saw a white Mercedes pull up in a gate layby nearby. At first I thought it was Donald's, but then I saw Stuart running across the wasteland that the shelter was situated next to. He ran up the steps and into the shelter. "Good morning, Lady Mc-Fadden. How did your welcome evening go?"

"Good, but you were missed. Could you not make it?" I asked.

"No. I told Donald to give you a message from me. Did you not get it?"

"Actually, yes. I did get it. Thank you, it was thoughtful of you."

"Did you take my advice and find yourself a cupboard?"

"Yes, but to be honest with you, I could not cry. I never cried at Thomas's death or his funeral, so having a cupboard has not been of any help to me." I could feel that I was becoming weepy. "You have such an emotional pull on me that all I have to do is look into your beautiful dark eyes, and I am transported to a very happy, loving place – one that I did not want Thomas to leave." That was it. I was blubbering all over again, and I could not stop myself.

"Please, Catherine, stop this crying. Not only are you upsetting yourself, but you are also upsetting me. It seems every time we meet, you have to cry!"

"Hold me please, Stuart," I asked quietly.

"I will if you stop this crying."

I felt his arms go around me. He pulled me towards himself. I could feel his heart beating, we were so close. I could smell him and feel his breath on my neck.

"Right, have you stopped crying now?" asked Stuart.

"Yes, of course I have. Sorry. I promise to try and control my outbursts. Please kiss me."

Stuart hesitated and then placed his lips hard against mine. It was only for a moment, but the passion went raging through me.

Stuart pulled away and started to discuss what he needed for the project on the stone shelter. "Just draw me some details of what you wish it to look like. There is not much can be done, as it is a listed building." With that, he ran off to his car.

I shouted, "Mr. Pennington, that was not a kiss!"

Stuart shouted back, "Mrs McFadden, I beg to differ. That was a kiss!" Then he was driving away.

I took my phone out to take some photos of the garden area around the shelter. I heard a car. Stuart's white Mercedes was reversing back along the small lane. He parked, jumped out, ran back across the wasteland, and took me in his arms. This time we kissed and kissed. I could feel his tongue on my lips and then against my tongue. I was so sexually excited, I could hardly catch my breath.

Suddenly, I was freed. Stuart again ran off to his car, shouting, "Catherine, that was a kiss!"

"Stuart that was definitely a kiss. Please, sir, could I have some more?"

Stuart was driving away. "Maybe. Now fuck off, Catherine!"

I was elated. I knew that I was beginning to see him as Stuart Pennington and not the memory of Thomas Hague.

I walked back to the manor. The dogs and I were wet through. When I entered the kitchen, Babs said that Donald had also come home cold and wet.

I ran upstairs. Donald was on our bed, reading. I jumped on him and kissed him. I wanted him to make love to me while I was feeling so sexed up. Donald took advantage of the situation, and I felt his penetration. Then I did something that was wrong, so very wrong – I closed my eyes and tried to think of Thomas.

It did not work. Donald was Donald and Thomas was Thomas. They were too different. There was no comparison.

I was horrified at what I had tried to do. I was embarrassed. I had no need to substitute anyone for Donald. He was loving and brilliant. I felt so guilty. How could I?

I promised myself that I would never do that again. I would make it up to Donald, even though he had not been aware of anything different.

The next day, after Donald had gone to work, I was still feeling disgusted with myself. I decided I was going to help Donald by visiting Sheila, to see if I could find out whether it was due to me that Donald had not been able to see his baby.

I went into Donald's address book and copied Sheila's address for the satnav. The address was in Cheshire. The drive would take three hours each way, but if I set off after I had had something to eat, I would be back by the time Donald came home for our evening meal.

I set off and called at a children's store where I bought a present suitable for a two-year-old. By lunchtime I had reached the house where Sheila was living. It was a Georgian-style modern detached house, just off the slip road for the motorway.

I did not hesitate in any way. I was determined to find out what the problem was. I knocked at the large front door, and straight away, the house-keeper answered. I told her that I had arranged to meet my friend Sheila, and that I had the toy Sheila had asked me to buy for Jack.

She invited me into the hall and asked for my name. As she walked away around the corner I quietly followed. The housekeeper entered a lounge where Sheila was seated, and I walked straight in.

"Before you say anything, Sheila, I want you to hear me out," I said politely.

"Get out of my house, now!" she shouted.

"I just want to talk to you civilly. We go back a long way and always with Donald as the common denominator. I have only come to ask you, with respect, is it because of me that you will not let Donald see his son?"

"Get out, Catherine! The last person I want to talk to is you! My business is Donald's business, not yours. Don't flatter yourself. It has nothing to do with you. Now leave!" I noticed from the way she was slurring her words that she was quite drunk.

"I implore you, please let me meet Jack while I am here."

"You must be joking." She got out of the chair she was in and fell to the floor. I quickly went to her aid, but she spat at me and screamed. I turned and left as quickly as I could.

The housekeeper was hovering by the door to the lounge. I asked her where baby Jack was. She told me they had a live-in nanny.

I ran to my car and drove away, straight up the slip road to join the motorway. I was really shaken up. I believed Sheila when she said that it was nothing to do with me. It was worth being spat at to have that confirmation.

The traffic and weather were really bad on the drive home. I seemed to have been on the roads for hours, and it was getting near to the time that Donald was due home. I was trying to work out what I had to tell Donald, but I need not to have bothered. My phone rang and over the hands-free connection, I had to listen to a verbal attack from Donald. I could not believe that he was speaking to me in that manner. After all, I was his wife.

"You can stop right there!" I shouted back. "I don't know what Sheila has told you, but I held no malice towards her or you. I needed to know that I was not the reason you were living in a painful situation."

"Get straight back here. You have to account for your inappropriate actions! I won't forget this, Catherine!" Then the phone cut off.

Babs and the staff had all gone home. I was tired and deeply upset by Donald's attitude. After parking the car, I walked slowly into the lounge. The dogs came to greet me. To my horror, Donald physically kicked them out of the lounge. They flew past me. Then I was angry. "What the hell is the matter with you?" I asked.

Donald grabbed my wrist and flung me onto the sofa. He shouted, "You stupid bitch! You had absolutely no right to meddle in my business. You have no right to rummage through my private papers to get Sheila's address."

There was pain in my wrist – Donald had twisted it as he flung me Enough was enough. This would be the last time my husband spoke to me like that, the last time he treated me like that. I did not need it. I did not want it.

"How dare you! Who the hell do you think you are? As your wife, I demand respect. I am not an employee or a clucking hen. I am the woman who loves you. I am your *wife*. And as of this minute, I do not want to be in your company. Fuck off, Donald!"

I picked up my car keys and left. I drove straight to the hotel and went into my office. As soon as I had settled down at my desk, I cried. I cried for Sheila, who was such a mess. I cried for me, who felt so lost again. What had I done that was so wrong?

I was cold, hungry, and tired after such a long day of driving. I helped myself to a few whiskies from the bottle in the office. Then I curled up on the very small sofa in the office and fell fast asleep.

It must have been about ten o'clock when Donald walked in, waking me up as he sat at my office desk.

"If you are going to start on me again, you can leave right now," I said quietly.

"They were only words, Catherine. I was so angry. I am sorry."

"If they were only words, then why is my wrist swollen and painful?"

Donald poured himself a whisky from the office bottle. There was silence between us for a long time. I did not want to speak. I was terrified that I would just burst into tears, and I did not want to ever do that in front of Donald. He was wrong. I had to be firm and strong if I was ever to stick up for myself.

At last Donald broke the silence. "Sheila told me that Jack is not my baby. She has since retracted that statement, but the seed of doubt is in my heart. We have argued and argued over all aspects of what we should do. She does not want me to have anything to do with Jack. I do not want anything to do with him either, but if the child is mine, I have a responsibility. I have asked her for a paternity test and she has refused. I have threatened to go to court to demand one. She said I can do what I want, but if a paternity test proves that I am not the father, then I should expect a scandal that the McFaddens will not be able to handle, especially my mother.

"Sheila is drunk most of the time, and maybe she is on drugs. There is usually a different male friend there every time I go. All we do is argue. I don't know what to do. I just want time to see if Sheila becomes more obliging. I do worry about the child, but there is a very good nanny there, and the housekeeper assures me that he is a happy, well cared for child.

"It is my belief that you should not be involved in my upset and heartache. I will sort this out, but not yet. If the child is mine, I will visit him. I will accept my responsibilities. But at the moment, I do not want the child to come and stay with us. I just want you, my beautiful wife, and soon a semi-retirement for us both. We will travel and live life to the full. I do not want to spoil that by having a child here."

All of a sudden, Donald burst into tears. I walked over to him and cradled his head against my chest. He sobbed out what sounded like an apology.

"Listen to me now!" I said sternly. "We are a team, a husband and wife team. What is yours is mine and vice versa. From now on, we talk things through and we do not keep any secrets. I will help you sort this problem. Please don't shut me out. And don't you ever disrespect and hurt me again, because I will not stand for it!"

"Get a room here at the hotel, Catherine. I need to hold you tonight. I think we both have had too much to drink to drive home."

I agreed. I arranged a room, and we retired for the night. We cuddled and held each other tight. Donald seemed so vulnerable. I felt such a love for him that night.

The next morning, we left the hotel very early. I wanted us to be back in the manor before the staff arrived. By breakfast, it was business as usual. Donald took me back to the hotel later so I could work for a few hours and collect my car.

I knew that I could not leave things as they were with regard to Jack. I went on the Internet and found a good, reputable paternity laboratory. After reading all the information on their website, I knew how to get the test done without anyone knowing. It stated that the mother's permission was not required, but the result would not be accepted by the courts. *Fine*, I thought, and I sent for their kit.

That night, after our evening meal, I told Donald what I had done. He was angry again, but he understood that we had to do something.

As he sat at his desk, sulking, I saw Sir Arthur in the far, right corner behind him. "Donald, please turn around slowly and look in the corner," I said.

"Oh, no, Catherine. Please say you are not going to bring me into your nonsense. Why can't you see that you are making yourself look like a fool? I have had enough!" He stomped out to his car and drove away, presumably to go to the pub for a drink.

I was not frightened by Sir Arthur. I had seen him appear and disappear so many times over the years that he did not bother me. What bothered me was that only I seemed able to see him. "Now look what you have done, Sir Arthur," I said. With a heavy heart, I retired to our room for a long, hot bath. I was fast asleep when Donald finally came home.

For the next few days, we hardly spoke to one another. We were angry and we were hurt.

After a day in meetings with the heads of departments at the resort, I came home to the manor. On Donald's desk, I noticed an envelope. The return address indicated it was the paternity test kit.

I opened it and read the instructions. It was so easy. All we had to do was provide two samples of DNA: one for the child and one for the father. Samples could be any sort of hair, saliva, or blood. These were to be returned with the fee, and results would be issued in a few days. The accuracy of this reputable laboratory was second to none.

Before she left for the day, Babs prepared a fantastic evening meal for Donald and me. When he came home, he showered and changed, and we sat down to enjoy the meal and each other's company. I poured us each some wine. After the meal, I took a big breath and mentioned that the test kit had been delivered.

I could see the look on Donald's face. Again, anger was there. He looked livid. "Show it to me," he said.

I brought it out, then realised he was too eager to get his hands on it. My best guess was that he would throw it on the fire if I gave it to him. I put it under my jumper and started to walk out of the room.

All of a sudden, Donald knocked me against the lounge door. I fell to the floor. What could only be described as a wrestling match for the kit ensued. I screamed with pain as Donald ripped my hand away from my jumper. He backed away. I got up and ran to our room. I locked myself in the bathroom.

I was angry. I had promised myself that I would never let him hurt me again. What was I to do?

"Catherine, come out. I am sorry. This has to stop. I am constantly fighting Sheila, and now it seems that you and I are always fighting. Have I hurt you? Please answer me. I am so sorry. To prove it, I will do the test. Tell me what you want me to do. Forgive me."

I came out, armed with a swab stick. I pushed it into his mouth and ran it over his inner cheek. I placed it in its container and fastened the lid.

"What do we do now?" said Donald.

"Leave everything to me. You do not need to do anything except make amends to me. I suggest that you bring the wine upstairs, get undressed, and wait for me." I laughed as I saw the expression on his face.

"On my way!" he shouted.

That night, I made love to Donald. I told him to just stay put until I finished with him. We laughed, we loved, and we enjoyed each other.

The following morning, I was a woman on a mission. I waited until Donald had left for the stables. Then, armed with the kit and a small pair of scissors, I set off to drive back to Cheshire.

I had no plan. I had no idea what I was going to do. All I knew was that somehow, I had to get a strand of Jack's hair. Maybe a hairbrush would do?

I drove all the way without taking a comfort break. I just wanted to get it over with. I would not rest until I got something of Jack's that would prove paternity.

I arrived in good time. I saw a young woman pushing a pushchair to-wards Sheila's house. Could it be the nanny with Jack? I parked up on the road and waited.

Sure enough, the girl pushed the pushchair into Sheila's drive. Then she stopped. She sat on the wall, laughing and talking on the phone. I was near enough to overhear; it sounded like she was talking to a boyfriend.

My mind was working overtime. What if I was to walk past them and then coo over the small child, all the while trying to cut a piece of his hair? No, that would not work. But I had to try something.

I got out of my car and slowly walked towards the girl. The nanny was so occupied in talking to her boyfriend, she didn't take much notice of me. Scissors in hand, I glanced at the sleeping child.

Oh my goodness – a dummy!

I slipped the dummy out of Jack 's mouth and went on my way. The nanny did not see. Jack carried on sleeping. I took out my own phone and, pretending to make a call, I snapped photos of the pair. Donald could confirm that the baby in the pram was Jack and the young girl was Jack 's nanny.

I walked straight back to my car. I placed the dummy in the specimen bag, sealed it, and drove away.

I had completed the paperwork beforehand, so all I had to do was close the envelope, take it to a post office, and send it recorded delivery. I chose a post office miles away from where we lived. I did not want anyone to recognize me.

I was pleased and relieved that the paternity test kit had been sent off. I decided that my next quest was to contact Stuart and tell him that I had com-pleted the sketches he asked for. Could he now help me more?

When I returned to the manor, I phoned the estate office and nervously waited for him to answer. When he did, I said, "Good afternoon, Mr Pennington. I have completed the sketches and was hoping you would have a look at them – not that you will – and perhaps you can do the plans needed – not that you will. What do you say? I know it is pointless, but I thought I would try."

"I have no idea who you are. I have no idea what you are actually asking for. Such negativity! Try again, Catherine!"

"Good afternoon Stuart. Catherine here. I have completed the sketches you asked for. I would be grateful if you could have a look at them, in order to draw up some plans and bills of quantities for the work at the old stone shelter. How was that? Was it good for you? It was good for me!"

We laughed.

"Meet me there in an hour. Is that all right?" asked Stuart.

"Oh yes, great! See you then."

I took the dogs from the back kennel and, armed with my sketches, strolled down the overgrown path to the stone shelter. Stuart arrived, and after glancing at my drawings, he took measurements with computerized measuring app.

"It is all done by lasers. You just take a picture, tell the computer where you want to measure, point, and shoot. Marvellous toy," said Stuart as he walked around the site.

I watched him very closely. He reminded me so much of Thomas, but that day I was watching him as Stuart Pennington. I found him very attractive.

Just as Stuart finished measuring the areas I had specified on my rough plans, it started to rain. We ran into the shelter, dogs and all.

"My, that was a stroke of luck. I can now complete your 3D plans and a bill of quantities for you to use at your leisure. I will make a list of our suppliers and arrange for the digger. The rest you should be able to do on your own. I am too busy to get involved – you do understand that, don't you?"

"Of course I do, and I am grateful," I replied.

I looked into his beautiful dark eyes. Stuart returned my gaze. Again I had no control of my stupid emotions.

"Stop it, Catherine! Don't you dare start crying! You wear me down. I suppose you want me to hold you again?"

I nodded, and then I felt his arms around me. He pulled me close to him. Without being prompted, his lips were heavy on mine. This time he did not stop kissing me. Instead he placed his hands under my jumper and held my breasts. He kissed me sensually, and his hands stroked and squeezed my breasts at the same time. It sent me to a place of memories belonging to the past. I was very aroused.

Stuart pushed me gently against one of the tall walls in the shelter. I could feel his manhood, and I knew that Stuart was also very aroused. I pulled him closer to my body. Talking through his kissing, Stuart whispered, "Take your pants and knickers down."

"No, Stuart. No!"

"I am not going to fuck you. I just want to feel you. I just want to feel you intimately." He pulled my clothing down and at the same time got hold of my hand and put it in his unzipped trousers. I felt his erect penis and stroked him. Stuart's hand slid between my legs, gently caressing me. My desire for him was unbearable.

Suddenly he pulled away and told me to adjust my clothing. He adjusted his own clothing.

"I need you to know that I love my partner Jonathon. I cannot keep doing this. I feel so guilty. I am sorry, Catherine!"

He then turned and walked off into the rain. I just stood there, wondering what the hell had happened. It would have been so easy for me to be unfaithful to Donald. Was that the reason why Stuart retreated?

I needed to walk. I needed to think about what had happened. What I did know was that Stuart Pennington made me feel good. Stuart, not Thomas. It was nothing to do with my beloved former husband.

By the time I reached the manor, the dogs and I were wet through. I put the dogs back into their kennel and went into the kitchen. Babs was busy preparing the evening meal. After making me a hot drink, she sent me upstairs to have a bath.

I decided not to tell Donald about the paternity test. I only briefly mentioned that Stuart was to arrange for a digger to clear the wasteland. Donald was not interested, so it suited me not to give him too much information.

That night I stared into a dark corner in the lounge. Sure enough, I began to see the smoky outline of Sir Arthur. Perhaps Donald was right, and it was my imagination that was bringing Sir Arthur to me.

I curled up on the sofa after Donald and I had eaten our evening meal. The dogs were dry by then, so they were allowed in the lounge by the fire.

"You are very quiet tonight, Catherine," said Donald.

"I am just tired and a little fed up."

"I think I have been neglecting you. Just let me get the lambing season out of the way, and I think we shall have the honeymoon we promised ourselves. Malta, yes?"

"Something needs to change, Donald," I observed.

"Don't be so dramatic. You have everything you ask for and more. You sound very ungrateful."

I fell asleep on the sofa. Donald carried me upstairs and put me into our bed. I felt quite sad. It had been such an emotional time over the past few days. I thought that once Donald had proof that Jack was his child, his attitude would be better.

A couple of days later, Babs came into the lounge, where I was doing some work on my computer. She brought me a note. "One of the groundsmen dropped this off for you."

I knew it was from Stuart. Obviously he did not want to deliver it himself. Probably he did not want anything more to do with me. He had told me over and over again that he had too much respect for his partner, Jonathan, to do anything that would hurt him, but I had taken no notice.

The note said that he had arranged for a digger to do the foundations, probably in a week or so. Well, that was something to look forward to.

A few days after that, I returned from my work at the Thistle Resort, and there on Donald's desk was a recorded delivery envelope. Babs had signed for it, but that was all right – there was no indication on the outside as to what it was. I waited patiently for Donald to come home.

I had only met the baby once before, and that had been on New Year's Day just over a year ago. I had been amazed even then at how much Jack was like Donald. He still was – a toddler with beautiful blue eyes and a head full of curly blond hair. I was so looking forward to Donald having the proof he needed that Jack was indeed his child.

That night Donald was late. He had been for a drink with his man friends and clucking hens straight from work. The lambing season was always hard, so I could not object to him having a drink or two. He left the car at the pub; one of his employees brought him home.

"I will heat our meal up and bring it to the lounge. Wine as well. Red or white?" I asked. I left the envelope where it could be easily noticed.

When I walked back into the lounge with the meal, Donald had already opened the envelope. He was staring at the contents. I was excited. "Well?" I asked. He did not answer. He gave me the results to read myself.

The paternity test proved that Donald could not be Jack 's father.

I burst into tears. How could Sheila have done this to him?

Donald took back the results and threw them on the fire. I watched as flames engulfed the papers. "Catherine, we shall never talk about this. You must forget what you know. When the time is right, I shall do something about it. Until then, I do not want to discuss it. Do you understand? This is not a game. This is a very serious matter. Again, do you understand?"

I nodded and dried my eyes. Neither of us could eat anything. Instead we drank too much and then curled up together in our marital bed.

I knew that Donald was devastated and heartbroken. Had I done the right thing by insisting on a test? I felt guilty thinking I had done the wrong thing, even for the right reasons. It was too late to do anything about it.

Over the next few days, I walked as on eggshells, trying not to do or say the wrong thing. When his mother came to see us on her weekly visit, she noticed something was off straight away. "What is the matter with you two? Is there something wrong?"

We reassured her that everything was fine. At least I was getting on better with her. I was civil, and his mother was charming towards me. The past was in the past, but what did the future hold for us all?

A few days later, another large envelope was delivered to me. This one came via groundsman from Stuart. He had done a wonderful job of producing six sets of plans, showing every detail that would be needed to build a garden and restore the old stone shelter. From the bills of quantities and list of suppliers, I was now in a position to choose and order materials.

A note said that the digger would be on site the following Tuesday, and the land clearance and dig out for the foundations would only take two days. That was as long as Stuart could spare the machine from other projects. He hoped I was well.

What on earth did Stuart mean by "Hope you are well"? Not a very serious consideration if he was having the plans delivered by a groundsman. He could have delivered them himself if he had wanted to know how I was.

The days that followed were full of a kind of silence. Donald and I had had a good love and contented marriage, but lately our closeness felt under threat. He was not so eager to play games with me or laugh with me or even make love to me spontaneously.

I knew that he had had a huge emotional shock. I knew what that was like because, after my beautiful Thomas had gone, nothing was ever the same again. I wanted to give Donald all my love and support. I knew that it would be some time before he was back to his arrogant, obsessive self. Donald had been there for me when I was at my lowest, and I intended to be there and help him through the heartache and anger he was feeling.

In fact, I knew that I loved him more than I had ever thought I could love him. The problem was that Donald was showing no interest in me and no sign of his love for me. I knew things would get back to normal, but how long it would take was anyone's guess.

Tuesday came, and sure enough, a digger was delivered to the bottom field. I heard the noise from the manor. I went off to work at the resort, looking forward to the start of the foundations for the stone walls and arch.

It was late afternoon when I received a phone call from Stuart. He rang the hotel's line. "Catherine, firstly, please give me your mobile number. I have been trying to contact you for the last hour."

I gave him the number and asked what I could do for him.

"Your excavation has stopped. You are not going to believe this, but they have found a human skeleton where they were digging. The police have been called. Also, with your permission, I would like to call Father Benedict. No one has to go near the site. The police will want to interview you, and I suppose me, at some time soon."

"Are you joking with me, Stuart?"

"No, afraid not! Once I get permission to remove the digger, I will have to take it to another job. It could be a long, drawn-out investigation, and it will probably be quite a while before you can restart your foundations."

We both went quiet. "Are you OK?" asked Stuart.

"I suppose so. I feel shocked and very sad. How long has the skeleton been there?"

"I have no idea. I don't know anything yet. I have been named as the main point of contact, so I will let you know whenever I hear anything." Another silence. "Do you fancy a cuddle?" whispered Stuart.

"Oh yes! Don't say anything else or you will have me crying!"

With that we said goodbye.

I phoned Donald at the stables, but they said he had not gone in to work that morning. I tried his mobile and it was switched off. I had no idea where he was. By that time, I was very angry. I phoned Babs and asked her if she had heard from him. She said she had not.

I then phoned Stuart back and asked him if he had told Donald about the skeleton.

"No, I have not been able to contact him. I'll speak to him later, when he returns from the auction."

"What auction?"

"A horse auction at the Lancastrian estate. He probably has his phone switched off."

There followed yet another silence.

"Well? What are you not telling me?" I asked.

"You are not going to like this, Catherine. I asked Donald to take Linda with him, so she could do all the necessary paperwork. Nothing sinister, I assure you."

I just turned my phone off.

I got into my car. It was the time that Donald usually went to the pub after work. I decided to go there to see if I could find out what the bloody hell was going on.

Donald's car was not outside the pub, but I went in anyway. I asked the bar staff if they had seen him, which they had not. But as I turned to leave, in walked Donald, talking and laughing with that Linda! He obviously had not seen my car, because he looked very surprised when he saw me.

I waited for either Donald or Linda to speak. It was a very awkward situation. I knew there had been something between them. I did not know what to do or say.

Donald was the first to speak. "I just bumped into Linda after I finished work, so I offered to buy her a drink. You don't mind, do you?"

"Has Linda been at the office all day?" I asked politely.

Linda chirped up, "Yes! I was looking forward to coming for a drink. We have been so busy."

I knew that Linda had not been at the office. Stuart had already told me where she had been. They were obviously prepared to lie through their teeth. I felt physically sick.

"Sit down, Catherine, and I will get you a drink," said Donald.

I sat down at the table with Linda. When Donald returned with drinks for us all, I said, "Neither of you has been in the office today. You were together. I would like to know why you have lied to me?"

No answer came. I could see the look of dismay on Donald's face. I stood up and excused myself. "Stuart told me, entirely innocently. He was looking for you. There has been an incident on our land, where the digger was working. You will need to sort it out, Donald. As for you, Linda, may I suggest that you find employment elsewhere?"

I drove straight home and was met by a number of police cars in our driveway. Stuart stood near the kitchen, at the back of the manor. One look into those beautiful dark eyes and I sobbed and sobbed inside.

"Why are you always so emotional, Catherine? There's good news. It seems the skeleton must be hundreds of years old. They have sent for representatives from the Edinburgh Museum; we will know more when they arrive. In the meantime, they have cordoned off the area. There will be some sort of archaeological dig to see what else they can find. You never know, there might be some Roman coins or the like." Stuart's tone was light.

"I have just seen Linda and Donald. I think that they

are having an affair," I whispered. "That is why I feel upset."

"People in glass houses comes to mind," Stuart observed.

I looked at him, and he winked at me. The cheek of him. Apart from a kiss and fumble, I had nothing to be ashamed of. Did he condone Donald's actions? That was the last straw!

I walked away into the manor. Nothing would ever be the same again. Even Stuart was only interested in what he could get or do.

Babs agreed to stay on later that night. There were so many people milling around, and all I wanted was to have a drink with Ruth at the hotel. I was just about to leave when Donald arrived home. I avoided him. I saw Stuart go into the lounge, where Donald was. They were having an argument. I moved closer to the door to listen to what they were saying.

"How dare you sack Linda?" Stuart shouted. "She will not be leaving. If you pursue this dismissal, then I will personally help Linda take you to the industrial tribunal, and I will make sure you are charged with sexual harassment. Linda can claim that you wanted sexual favours in exchange for her employment, and I will personally enjoy seeing you get what you deserve!"

There followed a scuffle, so I walked in to calm the situation. Donald had Stuart pinned against the wall. They could not see me. Stuart said, "You are a bastard the way you treat women. You can't even treat your new wife with respect, and it is obvious you just don't do it for her!"

I froze. What was Stuart doing? He had sworn that he would never tell anybody about what we had done.

At that moment, both men saw me standing there. They separated. Donald spoke, but I was not interested in what he was saying. I just looked into Stuart's eyes and then turned and walked out of the manor.

I got into my car and went to the hotel to meet Ruth. I needed a friend to talk to, and Ruth loved listening to other people's problems. Armed with two large whiskies, we made ourselves comfortable in a small lounge.

My phone rang. It was Stuart. I answered it and said, "I thought you were about to tell Donald. Why? If you had not seen me there, you would have told him, wouldn't you? I really trusted you, Stuart. I have been so wrapped up with my emotions over Thomas, I did not see you for what you are. Don't worry. I will never let Jonathan know what a two-faced cheater you are. I think we are done now, don't you?" I turned my phone off.

Ruth and I had a few more whiskies and were really enjoying ourselves. Then Stuart walked in and sat next to me. He told Ruth she was needed somewhere else. Ruth took the hint and left the room.

"I know that you will never forgive me," he said earnestly, "but I would never have said anything more to Donald. My temper just got the better of me. Donald and I have some bad history from when we were younger. We are OK now. I don't want to lose your friendship. I love the feel of you. Do you want a cuddle now? And … maybe you could ask me to kiss you, and then I can touch you?"

I laughed. "All right, Mr Pennington, you have made your point. To put the record straight, I would love a cuddle, a kiss, and a feel. I would *really* like you to make love to me, but that bit will never happen."

We were laughing when another voice came from the doorway. "What are you doing here?" said Donald.

Neither Stuart nor I answered him. I wondered if my husband had overheard my words, but what the hell. At that moment, I genuinely did not care.

Stuart said goodnight and left. Donald let him pass and just glared at me. "You had better tell me what is going on."

"I don't think you are in a position to ask anything of me. But if you want to know something I will tell you, then I think the skeleton is that of Sir Arthur. I intend to do everything in my power to find out what year he might have been from and whether there was any leather or metal clothing. I am going to ask the museum staff to let me know all of their findings. If there is a chance that it is Sir Arthur, I am going to ask Father Benedict to contact the bishop, and I am going to arrange for Sir Arthur to have a burial in the grave-yard near the chapel.

"Do you remember the chapel? It is where you took an oath to love me and protect me and be faithful to me. I have always been faithful to you. I might have been a little naughty and flirtatious, but I have never been unfaith-ful. I will be staying here tonight. I want nothing to do with you."

I had to stop because my tears had started.

"I have not been unfaithful," Donald declared. "I admit the excursion started out as an opportunity to have a bit of sex fun with Linda, but I have not had sex with her, I swear. I know you won't believe me. After I told Linda she no longer has employment with me, I doubt she will back me up either. But this is the truth: I took her to the Lancastrian estate as I needed to sort some breeder's papers out. I also went to an estate agency and asked them to sell your house. They have given me all the necessary papers for you to sign, and they need a set of keys as soon as possible. Forgive me. I need you more now than I have ever needed you."

"Good night, Donald. I am staying here tonight. There are many peo-ple around the manor. Please make sure all our belongings are safe." I turned away from him, and I heard him leave.

The next morning I woke in one of the hotel's bedrooms. I was sur-prised that I had not got a massive hangover, as I had drunk a considerable amount of whisky. At breakfast, I laughed at Ruth. She was classically hung-over.

"You seem very happy this morning," Ruth said.

"Actually, I feel really good. I'm looking forward to finding out about the skeleton buried on our land. I am also looking forward to Donald making it up to me. I believe him, and I know that he is in a very bad place. I know he needs me by his side and in his bed. I am looking forward to our future."

I returned to the manor at lunchtime. Donald was not there. He returned about two o'clock. He seemed very flustered. "Catherine, I think I have done something stupid. I have been to see Sheila. We argued and argued. Sheila went for me, and I hit her. She collapsed on the floor. I think that I hurt her. The housekeeper was screaming at me. I just left and drove home. If Sheila contacts the police, I am in great trouble."

"Could it be classed as self-defence? Do you think you should call your lawyer friend and tell him what has happened so he can advise you? Did you tell Sheila that you knew that Jack was not your son?"

Donald had not let Sheila know that he had had a paternity test. He told Sheila that, because of the seed of doubt she had sown, he wanted to have a test overseen by the court. He claimed he had said this only to see what her reaction would be.

She was already quite drunk, and it was not even lunchtime. She had started shouting and swearing. Then she flung herself at Donald, spitting and hitting. That's when Donald had struck her. The housekeeper had witnessed it all.

Donald had had a very bad few weeks. He looked lost. He took my hand and kissed it. "I want to take you to bed with me now. I need to hold you and make love to you, my wife."

"I could do with some afternoon delight myself. Come on, Squire. Even just cuddling will do it for me."

"Oh no, I need more than that."

We went to our room and stayed there all afternoon. In the early evening, Babs knocked on our bedroom door. "Squire, the police are here to see you."

"All right. I will be down in a moment." We got dressed quickly and went downstairs.

The police officers introduced themselves as from Edinburgh police station. They said that they had been sent in to speak with Donald because of the locally sensitive nature of the investigation. They asked Donald to accompany them to the station to answer questions regarding his ex-wife Sheila.

Donald agreed. One of the officers commented that Donald had probably been one of the last people to see his ex-wife alive.

I screamed, "What? What are you saying? How dare you not tell us about what has happened to Sheila? When did she die? How did she die?"

Nobody answered me. Donald appeared to be in shock. The police officers took him away. I found the solicitor's phone number and called it.

What followed was the longest night ever. I could not sleep. I lay on the bed, waiting for someone to phone me. Nobody did.

Had Donald hurt Sheila more than he thought he had?

I waited for dawn to break. Then I showered, got dressed, and made myself ready to go to the Edinburgh police station. The more I thought about going there, the more the idea seemed wrong. I changed my mind, deciding to wait at home until someone contacted me.

By just after breakfast, all the vehicles and personnel involved with the stone shelter site had left. The manor and its immediate grounds were quiet.

A representative from the museum called to tell me that they had erected a large tent on the waste ground adjacent to the dig. They had full access from a small road well away from the manor proper, so we would not be disturbed any more.

I asked, "Who is the person in charge of the whole operation?" I was told that it was a Professor Roberts.

All morning I paced up and down the kitchen or immediately outside. Babs kept telling me that I should eat something. I felt ill with hunger, but I could not eat.

Just after lunchtime, Donald walked into the kitchen. All I could see was a tall, beautiful man with curly blond hair and wonderful blue eyes. He was my husband, and I looked straight into his eyes.

Neither of us said anything. I put my arms around his neck, and he put his arms around me, pulling me in as close as he could. We were cheek to cheek; I could feel his breath on my neck. We held each other tightly, and delicious sexual feelings racing through my body.

"I love you more than I ever thought I could," I whispered to him.

"Well, my Mrs McFadden, I cannot tell you how much I love you, want you, and need you. You are my whole life!" He kissed my neck. "Sheila fell to her death from the motorway bridge near her home. She could have been pushed or she could have jumped."

I was shocked but I kept hold of Donald tightly. His body shook, and I could hear him sobbing quietly. He continued, "Before the incident, Sheila was seen arguing with a man on the bridge. The police thought that I was that man. I had stopped for petrol on the way home, and the police managed to secure CCTV footage from that garage. I was at there at the exact time Sheila fell. They are looking for someone else for the murder, but they have charged me with assault based on the witness statements from Sheila's housekeeper and the nanny."

We held each other for quite a while. Donald stopped sobbing and tried to compose himself.

Babs started clanging around the kitchen, making Donald something to eat. Then – the last thing we needed – his mother and Peter walked in, demanding answers. Inevitably, there were many rumours going about.

Donald did not let go of me nor I of him. "Where are all the people who were here yesterday?" he asked. I told him what I had been told: we would not be disturbed again.

Donald let go of me then and said, "I am going to shower and change. When I return, I will talk to you all." He looked at Babs. I remarked that Babs was one of us and she was loyal and discreet.

I would not say anything after that. I waited for Donald to return. When he did, we all sat at the large kitchen table. Babs offered us food, but only Donald wanted anything.

He told his mother and Peter everything he had told me. His mother and Babs started to cry. When he had finished talking, he ate his food in silence. Still terribly upset, his mother insisted that he go and collect the child. But she stopped crying after Donald told her the truth – that he was not Jack 's biological father. There was a deafening silence.

When Donald had finished, he said to me, "I am going to see Sheila's parents. I need to make sure that they and Jack are all right. I need to tell them the truth, so we can move on and make proper arrangements for the child. Do you want to come with me?"

I said he would do better on his own with them, and I would be waiting for him when he returned. Donald picked up his car keys and left.

Donald's mother turned to me and said, "I thank God that Donald has a woman like you at his side. When he returns, please ask him to contact me." Then she and Peter left.

CHAPTER 8

Sir Arthur

I collected my coat and walked out of the kitchen. Babs was crying, but I could not console her. I was too emotionally upset myself.

I took the dogs from their kennel and walked with them down the overgrown path to the dig. When I arrived, I could see the site was taped up and secure. Six or seven people were digging away, removing things, and placing them into small boxes.

I walked around the tape and entered the large tent. "Professor Roberts?" I asked.

"Yes, can I help you?" she replied.

"I am Catherine McFadden from the manor. I would like to know how long it will take before you have some idea of who or what you found here? I would really appreciate it if you could keep me informed."

"There are many tests to be conducted, and I am afraid it is very time-consuming. It will not be long before we have all the material dug out, however, and then you will have your place back," answered the professor.

"I think the remains are from the thirteenth century. Maybe an English soldier. In particular, please let me know if you find a helmet with a nose protector or a doublet made from woven metal."

"Are you interested in history, Mrs McFadden?"

"No, but I have done some research." I turned and started to leave the tent. "Thank you and goodbye, Professor Roberts. By the way, I called him Sir Arthur."

"I think I know where you are coming from."

I nodded and left.

I walked with the dogs along the roadway, a circuitous route to the manor. It was quite a way, but I needed some time to myself. I needed to cry for Sir Arthur, for Sheila, for Donald, and for myself. I had never felt so sad, not even for my beautiful Thomas.

As I entered the drive to the manor, I saw Donald's car. I took my time, composing myself. As I neared, I saw he was still sitting in the driver's seat. He rolled down the window and said, "Come on, Catherine. I am going to take you into the country and find us a quaint country pub. There I am going to treat you to a really good evening meal. What do you think?"

"That sounds so good," I replied.

"No need for you to change. Just jump in and let's go."

We had a wonderful evening. It gave us time to talk and reflect on everything that had happened. Donald had told Sheila's parents about his arrest and his alibi. He broke the news that he was not Jack 's father and expressed the hope that they would apply for legal guardianship of Jack.

He assured them that he wished to be known as an uncle and I as an aunt. He would always look after Jack 's well-being and support him. When this difficult period was over and Jack was older, Donald said he might try to have more contact with him.

After the funeral, he would ask his lawyers to get involved, to produce all the legal documents required for the courts.

Sheila's parents agreed in principle with what Donald said. They firmly declined his offer of assistance with the funeral arrangements.

That night Donald and I cuddled together, knowing that in the coming weeks we were in for a very bad time.

Sheila's funeral came and went. Donald kept his word with regard to contacting his lawyers. Sheila's parents became Jack 's legal guardians. Donald would be noted on the birth certificate as not the child's father. Financial arrangements were made for Jack's upbringing and education. It all seemed so clinical but that was what Donald wanted.

Eventually the Crown Prosecution Service decided not to prosecute Donald over the assault. There were sufficient grounds for a self-defence plea.

The Edinburgh Museum's team of archaeologists closed down their dig. I was looking forward to their findings. I had not seen Sir Arthur since the day the digger unearthed the remains. That was one reason why I believed the skeleton was that of Sir Arthur.

I was so relieved to be able to stand, quiet and alone, in the old stone shelter and looked forward to continuing where I had left off. I wanted to restart the work before autumn.

My first job was to get that bloody digger back. I knew I would have a difficult time persuading Stuart Pennington to give it up. I took a deep breath and phoned the estate office. I presumed that it was Linda who answered, and I asked her to put me through to Stuart. She must have told him that it was me on the phone. "Well, so you are back, Catherine. How are you?" he said.

"I am fine, and how are you?"

"OK. I suppose you want me to give it to you?"

"Yes, I do," I answered, trying not to laugh.

"Have you been looking forward to me giving it to you?"

"Oh yes, I have. The sooner the better, please."

"It will give me great pleasure to give it to you. Now, what about the JCB digger?"

"That as well would be great!" I said. "Would tomorrow be too soon?"

"I will probably be able to get it there for you to have for two days – but only two days. Now, do you fancy having lunch with me? I will take you to the large building suppliers. You can choose your bricks for the raised flower beds and the gravel for the surrounding paths."

"Yes, that sounds wonderful."

"Right. I will pick you up in about an hour."

"See you then," I replied.

I rushed around, trying to make myself look really good. Stuart arrived and I got into his car. "You look well, Catherine," he said.

As usual, the delicious sexual feelings were all over my body. I was so pleased to be with him. I knew that it was wrong of me to keep playing this dangerous game, but I convinced myself that it was harmless fun.

Stuart was the perfect gentleman. He took me to the building suppliers, and there I chose red bricks and a mixture of red, pink, white, and cream quarry gem stone for the surrounding paths.

"And now I suggest that we go and have some lunch," said Stuart.

He drove us to an Italian restaurant situated on a riverbank. It was a hot day, so we settled at an outside table, and Stuart ordered loads of finger foods. We drank lime and lemons. Stuart said if we did not drink them, we could always use them as fingers bowls.

"You have had a really bad time, haven't you? Do you want to talk about it?" he asked.

"No. Everything is getting back to normal now. It is Donald who has had to deal with the most traumatic events – but as I said, things are getting back to normal."

"Is it true that he has been charged with attempted murder?"

"Good grief, no. Who told you that nonsense?"

"There are many rumours going about. Forgive me for listening to them. I admit, I would have loved for him to be charged with attempted murder, but you can't always get what you want."

I recoiled. "Why did you say that?" I demanded.

"Sorry, Catherine. I should not have said it. Don't mention this conversation to Donald; he might get the wrong idea."

"What idea?"

"Many years ago, Christine, Donald's first wife, died in a tragic riding accident. I blame him for her death. He said that he had phoned for an ambulance, but there was no record of that call. By the time someone else called, she was dead. I know that Donald wanted Christine dead. And you are very much like Christine. Sorry! Please forget all this nonsense."

I stared at him.

"Forget it," he repeated. "Now come on. I need to contact your bricklayers to tell them your site will be ready in a couple of days from tomorrow.

Make sure you have got the stone mason on your site as soon as possible. He will order his own material. Before we go, I want to suck your fingers clean, and you can do the same for mine. Any chance?"

"Nope!" But the thought really turned me on.

That night I showed Donald a sample of the brick and a sample of the gravel. He was not amused at me having gone out with Stuart. "Don't trust him, Catherine!"

"Why?" I asked. "You employ him in the highest position on your estate. Why do you not trust him?"

"I don't trust him with you."

"I thought he was gay. He calls Jonathan his partner."

"Have you ever heard of being bisexual? It means no sexual preferences. Male or female. That is why I do not want you to trust Stuart Pennington."

The following morning, I was scheduled to visit the local primary school. I was just leaving the manor when Donald said that a Professor Roberts wanted to speak to me on the phone.

"Good morning, Lady Catherine. This is a courtesy call to tell you that we have finalised our findings on the dig. I thought you might be interested to know what they are."

"Oh yes!" I replied.

"You were absolutely correct with your dates. The remains were carbon dated to the thirteenth century, within a range of error, of course. The artefacts were clothing, men's clothing, including a helmet and reinforced body armour. We did not find any weapons, say a sword or dagger. The historical record isn't definitive, but he may well have been a member of the English army, retreating from Scotland."

"Thank you so much. You have no idea what this means to me," I said. "I now have a responsibility to make sure that Sir Arthur, as I call him, is brought back here and buried in consecrated land. I would appreciate any help you could give me with regard to the logistics."

The professor understood exactly what I was asking of her. In due course, she arranged the logistics of bringing Sir Arthur back to the estate to be buried.

I told Father Benedict the whole story of Sir Arthur, and how our connection had spanned quite a few years. He recalled me asking him to look in the chapel records to confirm that a priest had conducted a rite at the manor.

I requested that Father Benedict obtained permission from the bishop for the remains of Sir Arthur to be buried in the graveyard by the chapel. I was passionate about laying Sir Arthur to rest in consecrated ground, so he could be at peace.

All this took time. With the work at stone shelter being done at the same time, I found myself so busy, I had no time for anything else. I told Ruth to do without me for at least a month, and she agreed to cover my resort responsibilities. Poor Donald must have been sick and tired of my goings-on.

Although I was always remembering Thomas, I did not get upset as much anymore. In fact, I was more upset at the thought of Sir Arthur dying. His poor family and friends probably never knew what had become of him. Was he an ordinary soldier, a knight, a lord, or maybe someone as famous as a king?

I was a romantic. I wanted to believe that the Lady Catherine McFadden of that time was the captive of the English knight Sir Arthur. They became lovers and were eventually separated by the Scottish laird when he took back his lands. Perhaps Sir Arthur was killed then — a love story with a terrible end-ing.

No one knew what had happened to his Lady Catherine. The only reference in the old records said, "Lady Catherine was placed in the castle's dungeon, where she lived, only brought out into the daylight when McFadden needed use of her." A very sad story.

Within weeks, the stone shelter was repaired and cleaned. Our gardeners filled the raised flower bed with soil and planted hundreds of heather plants, all different colours. Thin conifers were planted on either side of the steps to the shelter, and between the stone benches that had been sited on the gem stone gravel. The path from the manor was cleaned up, the joints between the stone flags filled. More heather was planted on each side of the path.

It was beautiful. I was so proud of it, and Donald was suitably impressed when he came to see the finished job.

After the completion, I met with Father Benedict, who by that time had received permission from the bishop to bury Sir Arthur in the graveyard. I asked Donald to come to the meeting, but he flatly refused.

I met Father in the graveyard, and between us, we chose a final resting place for Sir Arthur. A burial service was arranged for the following week.

Knowing that I only had a week to obtain a headstone, I immediately went to the stone mason's shop. They said that they would do their best to deliver it the following week. I wrote the following wording for the engravers:

> *Here lies Sir Arthur, a name adopted for time to come,*
> *Who died over six hundred years ago,*
> *Now buried in consecrated ground.*
> *Rest in Peace, Sir Arthur.*
> *Love from Lady Catherine McFadden.*

At last I could relax. I arrived home, pleased with myself.

Donald was in a terrible mood. I asked him what on earth was the matter with him, and he said that he was bored, fed up, and miserable. He accused me of being selfish, always thinking of myself and what I wanted. He suggested that we should just set off and have the honeymoon we had promised ourselves for so long.

I agreed in principle, and said that after Sir Arthur's burial service, we could fly out to Malta for a couple of weeks.

Donald just went mad. He shouted at me, telling me that we should go to Malta immediately. He was demanding that I miss the most important thing in my life at that moment. I refused and insisted that I wanted to see Sir Arthur laid to rest.

"Your imagination will get you into trouble one day, and I won't be there to protect you. You should have more sense at your age! Can you not see that there is no connection between your rantings about a ghostly figure, and a dead body that has been buried for hundreds of years? All coincidences and nothing more. We leave now or there will be trouble between us. I have had enough of your stupid games!"

Donald pushed past me, knocking me against the door as he stormed out of the manor. He drove away at speed and left me standing there, wondering what the hell had happened.

I collected the dogs and made my way slowly down the stone path to the new rose garden. I sat in the beautiful stone shelter, and all I could think of was Sir Arthur being buried there all those years. He had been alone. I truly believed that he chose me to help him get peace and move on.

I was upset by the way Donald had belittled me, and I was upset at the thought of Sir Arthur. I just wanted to cry and cry. I sat with my face in my hands, and I did cry. I felt miserable.

Arms came around me. From the sexual thrill that followed, I knew it was Stuart Pennington by my side. "Hey, what is the matter, Catherine? Is this where you've found a private space to grieve for Thomas? It is truly beautiful and a credit to you. Do you want me to leave you alone?"

I tried to calm myself by taking deep breaths. "No. I-it's not what you think," I hiccupped.

"Come here. Let me hold you. If that is what helps you, I don't mind holding you until you feel better."

The sensual feeling of his arms around me was wonderful. "Kiss me, Stuart," I asked.

"Not a good idea."

"*Please* kiss me, Stuart."

His lips were on my lips, heavy and sensual. I kissed him back. Before long we were kissing each other like lovers do.

Stuart stood me up and put me against the tall wall of the shelter. What happened next could only be described as heavy petting. Stuart touched me intimately and I touched Stuart intimately. In a way, we satisfied each other sexually. I did not want him to leave me. Afterwards we held each other close, as if we were truly lovers, but without the sexual intercourse.

"I told you it was a bad idea, did I not?" Stuart laughed.

"You did, and I enjoyed every minute. I could even do it all over again."

"The problem with you, Catherine, is that you are greedy. You don't know when you have had enough." We giggled and kissed, and I felt so much better.

"I have to go," Stuart said. "Are you all right now?"

"Yes, thanks to you," I replied.

"This will not do, Catherine. One day I will not stop, and I will end up fucking you. That will be like committing career suicide for me and marriage suicide for you. That must never happen. Are you listening to me?"

"Of course I am. I promise I will not put you in that position again," I said – and then I laughed.

"Not funny, Catherine. Not funny!" Stuart ran off to his car, which was parked in the layby. I walked back to the manor.

I told Donald again that I was not going to be blackmailed into missing Sir Arthur's funeral service. I had worked too hard to give it all up at the last minute because Donald was so selfish and demanding. Donald sulked and ignored me for the rest of the week.

The day finally arrived for the funeral of Sir Arthur at the chapel. Donald refused to go, so it was just Father Benedict and me in attendance. I had thought Professor Roberts would be there, but she was not. It was a short service but a pleasant one. That is, if you can say that "very, very sad" is pleasant. The stone mason placed the headstone, and I cried.

Afterwards I walked around the small graveyard. It was a beautiful place. I saw the gravestone dedicated to Christine McFadden, wife of the Squire Donald James McFadden. It made me physically sick, as it did each time I saw it. I then made my way back to the manor.

I changed into my riding gear and walked to the stables. I took the dogs with me. I knew that I would have to make more of a fuss of Donald. Like any male, he could be childlike if he did not receive the right sort of attention. I realised that perhaps I had been too preoccupied of late. A little more romance, sex, and love would probably do us both a world of good.

As I entered the stable yard, I was met by the pigs, Butch and Spoilt. I laughed as the dogs, Jeremy and Jess, backed away, looking scared to death. The pigs chased them, making the situation a lot worse.

As I called for the pigs to come to me, they turned and charged, knocking me to the ground. They were only small, about the size of our dogs but they were very strong. What made it even worse was that they loved to be petted. As they jumped around and sniffed at me, I could not get back to my feet properly.

One of the stable girls came to my aid. My dogs had run away down the stable yard, where they were actually hiding!

Once I was upright and composed, I saw the funny side of it all, and I laughed and laughed. I needed to laugh. I had been far too serious for quite some time.

"Where is the squire?" I asked the stable girl.

"He is at the breeding stables. Do you know where they are, Lady Catherine?"

"No. I have been there, but I cannot remember how to get there."

"They are about two miles along this road, or you can walk or ride there by the country road at the bottom of the yard."

"Can you tack my horse up? I will enjoy riding there with the dogs."

"Yes, Lady Catherine. It won't be long." She went to get my horse ready. When she returned, leading the mare, I took the horse to the mounting step and swung up in the saddle. I was a little nervous at riding by myself along a strange way, but I knew that I had to start making an effort. Off I went down the country path, Jeremy and Jess following me.

I reached the breeding stables in no time at all. Someone opened the large gate, and I rode in with the dogs still behind me. "Bloody hell, Catherine! Get those dogs out of here!" shouted Donald.

I turned my horse round and rode back out of the gate. The dogs followed me. When I was a safe distance from the yard, I dismounted and waited for Donald to come to me.

When he finally came, he was most apologetic. "Sorry, Catherine. We have been trying to get a bloody awkward stallion to mount a mare. He wants nothing to do with her. We have tried everything. Don't ask!" he added. "He is frightened around dogs.

"Anyway, aren't you being brave coming here on your own? Why have you come?"

Donald's attitude was terrible to me. I could remember a time when he would have been thrilled and loving if I had done something spur of the moment.

"Do I have to have a reason to come and see you?" I asked.

"I am very busy, and I do not have time to play games. I shall see you later, after I have been for a drink with William." And then Donald ran back to the stable buildings.

I was furious. I was not going to let Donald get away with treating me like an imbecile. I rode my horse back to the main stables and then returned to the manor with Jeremy and Jess.

It was a Friday night. Ruth was having a milestone birthday night out. She had booked a minicab for her ten guests, their destination the casino and nightclub in town. I phoned her and asked if she would mind me joining her birthday bash. She was delighted.

I phoned Donald and asked him to take me to the hotel before he met up with William. Then I rushed around getting ready. I wanted to show him I could look like a million dollars.

He came around to the manor at the appointed time, and I jumped in his car. He did not seem to notice me.

"It was very sad today, at the chapel with Father Benedict," I said. "We buried Sir Arthur, and that is why I wanted to see you. I needed you to comfort me but you could not be bothered with me."

"Don't be so soft, Catherine. It is not like you. I will see you later!"

We had arrived at the hotel. I got out of the car, and Donald just drove away.

I joined the other ten ladies, and the minicab whisked us away. We were told to meet it at eleven o'clock for our return journey. He told us he would not wait for anybody.

We had a wonderful meal. After an hour in the casino, we made our way into the nightclub. A fantastic band was playing. I adore trumpets and was thrilled to see this band had a full complement of wind instruments, especially trumpets.

I made my way to the front and settled myself at the side of the stage. I had lost the other women, but I just wanted to watch and listen to the band.

At the interval, I looked around for the others. All of a sudden, I saw Stuart Pennington standing at the far side of the room. As I saw him, he saw me. We acknowledged each other. Then I saw that Stuart was with a woman. She was all over him. I was a little jealous, and I was embarrassed at being so.

The band started up again, and Stuart came over to me. He took my hand and we walked onto the dance floor. I loved the feeling of him holding me. I loved looking into his dark eyes. I loved the smell of him. Stuart made me remember a happier time full of hope and excitement.

That time had been when I was with my beautiful Thomas. I was doing my best to get over his death. But Stuart reminded me so much of him that I felt Stuart as I had felt Thomas. I knew it was wrong, but I could not help myself.

We danced and laughed and I asked him, "Well, who is the woman?"

"A very close friend."

"I thought I was your close friend."

"No, you are my *best* friend. Is that OK with you?"

"Yes, I suppose so."

Suddenly I realised that it was later than I had thought. It was after eleven o'clock. "Sorry, Stuart; I have to run. I think I might have missed my lift home." I ran off to the back exit to see if the minicab was still there. No such luck. I looked at my phone and saw six missed calls. Just then Ruth called again, and I explained that I had not realised the time.

"We are on the motorway now, so we cannot circle back. Can you get a taxi and make your way back to the hotel? We are having a continuation party there. See you soon!" said Ruth.

I stood there with no idea where a taxi rank would be. A large car pulled up beside me, and a couple of men offered to take me for a ride. I ignored them and started to walk away. One of the men jumped out at me. I turned and bumped straight into Stuart.

"On your way, lads. There is nothing for you here!" shouted Stuart. The men drove away. "What on earth are you doing in this back- car park all on your own? You are asking for trouble!"

"Thanks, Stuart. I am so glad you were around. I have missed my mini-cab lift home. I have to get a taxi from the rank now."

"You have no chance at this time of night! You will be queuing for hours. You had better share the taxi that we have already booked."

When we returned to the nightclub, Jonathan was there with a woman. Stuart's close friend was also there. Stuart introduced me and then went to buy me a drink. When he returned, I told him that I wanted to sit at a table near the band; I did not want to be a gooseberry with the four of them. Stuart laughed, but I went anyway to find myself a table.

I stayed there until Stuart came to collect me. Their taxi had arrived. I insisted in being seated in the front of the taxi. No way did I want to sit with the four of them. Ugh!

All the way back to the hotel, I could hear kissing behind me. Donald was right. The men must be bisexual. I honestly did not understand that, but live and let live, Donald used to say.

I was glad when at last the taxi reached the hotel. I said thank you and goodnight to everyone, and ran in to rejoin the party.

Wow! The noise and laughter were so loud that I was thrilled to be there. I walked from the reception into the bar and restaurant. There were hundreds of balloons. Bottles of champagne and wine were open on all the tables. I did not want to know where the girls had got them from, and I did not care.

The chef had done us all proud: plain food, fancy food, spicy food, not to mention cake, fruit, and cream galore.

I saw Ruth climbing onto a table top. When she finally reached her goal and started to dance, she fell off onto the floor. Up she got again and once again tried to dance, only to fall off onto the floor again. A third time she got up – but this time we stopped her. We were all laughing. It was very funny, but she could have done herself an injury.

The music was very loud. Most of the hotel guests were there, dancing and singing. A gentleman asked me to dance, and I accepted. I decided to dance the night away. I jived, twisted, and line danced. I was a little drunk, but I was so intent on having a good time that I did not care.

I turned around and saw Stuart Pennington watching me. I went straight over to him. "Have you come to party?" I asked.

"Yes, I think I will join in. I have already had a good drink of champagne at the bar."

"What about your close friend?"

"Jonathan will entertain both ladies," whispered Stuart.

"Ugh! Too much information!" I replied, pretending to be sick.

Stuart put his arms around me, and we danced together. Those delicious feelings were back." Come into the garden with me," I whispered.

"OK. I will take a bottle of champagne with us." Stuart picked up an open bottle from one of the tables.

Hand in hand, we walked down the steps into the garden. Of course I had to stumble as I exited the building. Stuart picked me up.

I took him across the garden to the sun lounge. Nobody saw us. They were all enjoying the party in the hotel.

Stuart bolted the door to the sun lounge, and we stood in one of the corners. We each had a drink of champagne from the bottle. I spilled it down the front of my dress.

Stuart put the bottle down. We started kissing, only this time we kissed with a purpose. We were both highly aroused. Stuart's hands were all over me, and my hands were all over him. Stuart put his hands up my dress. After playing with my suspenders, he pulled my knickers down and I stepped out of them. He placed them in one of his pockets. He then undid his trousers.

"Catherine, yes?" he whispered.

I was not sure if we should.

"Catherine, yes?" he whispered again. "I will ask you one more time. Yes?"

"Yes!" I replied.

What followed next was superb intercourse. We were so aroused that I had no difficulty in having a fantastic orgasm, and then I felt Stuart climax. In the afterglow, we kissed and held each other close. I had no feelings of guilt. I was thrilled that we had finally made love to each other.

"Making love to you was brilliant, but you must never tell anybody about this," Stuart said urgently. "I mean it! This is serious; it is not a game. You and I must never talk about this, ever. You must forget it ever happened."

I just answered, "Yes."

My phone rang. One of the hotel receptionists was on the line. "Catherine, the squire is here. Where are you? He is waiting with a taxi at the front."

I quickly straightened myself, as did Stuart. I undid the door, then turned to Stuart and said, "I will not forget our lovemaking. Also, I want you to know that I was not making love to Thomas. I was making love to Mr Stuart Pennington."

"Yes, I know." As I left, he added, "Catherine, you are my best, best friend!"

As I had fallen down the steps on the way into the garden, so I fell up them going back into the hotel. As I passed through the party, I deliberately spilled whisky on my dress to disguise any telltale signs of what I had been up to. I also rubbed some cake into my neckline.

I ran out of the hotel, and Donald opened the back door of the taxi for me. He sat in the front. We were home in just a few minutes.

As Donald raided the fridge with the help of the dogs, I ran upstairs, calling back to Donald, "I am just going to change out of these clothes, as I have made a mess of them. Please fix me a large, milky coffee."

I showered thoroughly and put a dressing gown on. I returned downstairs, where Donald and I curled up together over a late supper.

My thoughts wandered to Sir Arthur. He was now at peace. Then I thought about Thomas. I was hoping I would never pine over him again. I knew he was at peace.

From that moment on, I had to show Donald how much I loved him.

CHAPTER 9

Final Commitments

From the night of Ruth's birthday, I found myself growing in emotional strength and self-confidence. I no longer pined for Thomas. I still thought about him, but I did not feel that I was heading down into a dark place full of anger and sadness.

I worked on proving to Donald that I could be the wife he wanted, and that I loved him more than I ever thought I could. Soon we were a close, contented, loving couple. I was beginning to feel like the old Catherine – the Catherine who was a very strong woman, who loved life and people.

I was happy at the manor. In fact, the manor was a very happy place to be. Donald's mother became a regular guest, and we got on well with each other. The duties I took on as lady of the manor became enjoyable.

At last Donald and I found time to have two weeks away in Malta as a belated honeymoon. We had a wonderful time. Every day was spent sightseeing. Every night was spent eating, drinking, and loving.

I had my family come to stay. I had promised them a holiday. I took my grandchildren pony riding. We all had a wonderful time. A week later, my sister Margaret and her husband had a holiday with us. Donald was charming to all my guests.

The first time I saw Stuart was at the stables. I was preparing to go out for a ride. Stuart had called to see Donald. When we bumped into each other, he greeted me with "Hello, my best, best friend."

To which I replied, "Hello to you, my best, best friend."

Stuart winked, I nodded, and I walked away. I could not believe the way my body tingled all over with sexual excitement. How unfair it seemed, but it could never be.

The second time I saw Stuart was when I went to pick Donald up at the pub after he had been drinking with all his man mates and clucking hens. I walked into the bar, and there was Stuart. We nodded to each other as I joined Donald in the other room.

"I am not ready yet. I will be another hour," said Donald.

"OK. I will come back for you."

"Never mind. I will come now, and we will take Stuart home."

As Donald, Stuart, and I went outside to the car, Donald changed his mind again. "I will stay a little longer. You take Stuart home and then come back for me."

Stuart tried to object, but he had no choice. As we got in the car, Stuart said, "How are you my best, best friend?"

"I am very well. And how are you, my best, best friend?" I replied, feeling rather cheated as those delicious sexual feelings surged through me.

I pulled up outside Stuart's large cottage. It was a beautiful place. "Do you want to come in? Jonathan is out at the moment," Stuart said.

"Do you want me to come in?" I replied.

"I want you to be strong for the both of us, as I am feeling very weak willed!"

"Then goodnight, Stuart!" I said.

Stuart got out of the car, and as he walked away, he shouted, "Goodnight, my beautiful Catherine!"

I drove away and returned to Donald in the pub.

Every so often, I would walk to the stone shelter and sit there, just enjoying peace and quiet. Sometimes I walked farther, to the graveyard where Sir Arthur was laid to rest. I would say a little prayer and talk to him.

Everything was going well between Donald and I. Then one day, it all changed. The summer had gone, and autumn had nearly ended. I returned home after a very busy day at the resort. Immediately I noticed that Donald's attitude had changed towards me. He had no time for me. Thereafter he avoided me, and at night he would not cuddle me. Over and over I asked him, "What the hell is wrong with you? What have I done?" He just ignored me.

This went on for a few weeks, and I was getting really upset. I began to think that perhaps he had fallen for another woman and no longer wanted me. I did not know what to do.

Then one Sunday morning, he said he was going for his usual ride. "Wait, and I will come with you. It has been a while since we have been riding together," I said.

"I would rather go on my own, if you don't mind."

"Yes, I do mind. I am coming with you. You and I need to have a very serious talk. I have had enough. I need an explanation as to why you are shutting me out of your life and hurting me so much."

Donald walked out of the manor. I followed him as he headed towards the stables. I phoned ahead to tell one of the stable girls to get my horse ready.

We walked in silence. When we reached the stable yard, Donald's horse was already waiting and they were just bringing my horse out. Donald mounted and went through the gate to the field. He left me. He never offered to throw me up and over, something he had always done for me. One of the stable girls offered to help me. Once mounted, I rode quickly after Donald.

I caught him up, and I was so angry, I just started to shout at him. "Right! I am not going to put up with any more of this. You had better tell me what the hell is happening between us."

"I know what you have done, Catherine."

I froze. I could feel my face flush. I felt sweaty and sick. "What do you mean, you know what I have done? Tell me what I have done, because I have not a clue what you are talking about."

He rode away from me, so I speeded up to catch him up. "Well?" I shouted. "Answer me!"

I was beginning to panic. Was he aware of what had happened on the night of Ruth's birthday? If he knew about it, I needed to put things right.

"How could you do it to me after all we have been through? Do you dislike me so much that you would hurt and humiliate me again?" shouted Donald, riding faster.

Again, I speeded up. "What the hell are you talking about? Please, Donald, talk to me. I need to put this right."

"I found your email – the email about purchasing a one-way flight to America. It was an open ticket for you to use any time. I knew that one day you would just fly to America, leaving me like you did once before."

I had no idea what he was talking about. I could not remember anything about a flight to America. I searched my memory frantically.

Then I remembered. Yes, I had purchased a one-way, open ticket to

America. It was when we were living at the hotel, before I moved into the manor. I purchased it on the morning that Donald's mother had come to see me. It had been Justin's idea, I recalled. He had seen the really good deal on the Internet. At the time, I was not in a good place, so I forgot all about it.

Donald was galloping fast down the fields. I knew he had completely got the wrong idea. The ticket was now out of date in any case.

I shouted to him to slow down. "You stupid man, how wrong you are!" I galloping after him.

Then Donald pulled his horse up, and I lost control of mine. My horse ran sideways into Donald's horse and veered towards the hedge. I saw a wooden fence in the hedge, and that was the last thing I remembered.

I woke up in a hospital bed. I thought I was in a dream. I could not lift my head off the pillow. In fact, I could not lift my arms or my legs. I called out for Donald. Where was he?

A nurse came over to me. "Lady Catherine, you are a very lucky lady. You have had a nasty fall, but you are all right. You have a gash on your head and are severely concussed. We sedated you, but you have no broken bones. Rest now. I will bring you a nice cup of hot, sweet tea."

"Where is my husband?" I shouted, but the nurse had left the room. I noticed that I only had a hospital gown on. Every time I tried to lift my head off the pillow, I went so dizzy that I became physically sick.

The nurse returned with my tea and helped me drink it out of a spouted cup. I asked her, "Where are my clothes? Where is my phone? Where is my husband?"

"Now calm yourself, Lady Catherine. Your clothes were cut off you, so you will need some more clothes. There was no phone with you when you were admitted. As far as your husband is concerned, no doubt he is on his way to sit with you. Now rest. The consultant will come and see you tomorrow. I will bring you something light to eat. Rest."

Again she hurried out of the room. It was going dark, so I knew it had to be about teatime. I found the bed buzzer. I pressed and pressed it until the nurse came back.

"Please phone my husband and tell him that he must come now to see me. Tell him to bring me some clothes. Tell him to come now!" I said.

Donald did not come that night. He left me all on my own. I needed to speak to him. I needed to put things straight. How dare he treat me like this? I was so angry and so upset, and on top of that I felt really poorly.

Every time I managed to get the nurse to my room, I asked her to phone Donald and let me speak to him, but that never happened. I needed a phone, but I could not get one.

I did not sleep at all that night. I watched the dawn break and remembered watching the same view from a hospital room in Los Angeles. I cried for Thomas. I cried for myself. I cried for Donald. I cried for Sir Arthur. I cried so much that my eyes were swollen shut. I could hardly open them in my swollen face. What a sight I must have looked.

At breakfast, a nurse got me out of bed and walked me to the toilet. As we returned, Donald was stood at the bedside. When the nurse had left, I looked at him and said, "Thank goodness you are here. Have—"

"I nearly killed you, Catherine. I nearly killed you! I cannot take any more!"

"Wait, Donald. I need—"

"I have packed up all your belongings and clothes and sent them to the Thistle Resort."

"Wait, you have it all wrong—"

"We are through, Catherine. I nearly killed you. Go and live the life you want. It is not with me!" Before I could say anything else, he had left the room.

I tried to get up off the bed and follow him, but I was too dizzy. I could not do it. I fell to my knees and cried.

The nurse returned and got me straightened around. "I need your help now," I said to her fiercely. "I will not take no for an answer. Please, please, get me a phone and the telephone number of the Thistle Resort. I urgently need to see my consultant."

The nurse looked angry and left the room. She returned with hot tea and toast for my breakfast. She also brought me a phone. "Hurry and make your call. Here is the number you asked for. That phone needs to go back!"

I rang the number and asked for Ruth. I was told that Ruth was not yet in. "Right, this is Lady Catherine. Now listen to me. I want you to contact Ruth and tell her that I am in the County Hospital. I am not sure what ward number. It is very important that she bring me a full set of clothes. They can be hers or she can buy me some. Tell her to bring them to me as soon as she can. It's really urgent. And tell her not to forget her phone. Did you get all that?"

The receptionist acknowledged that she knew what to do. I finished the call and gave the phone back to the nurse.

I waited and waited for Ruth and my consultant. I managed to sit in a chair and go to the toilet on my own. I was still uneasy on my feet and very dizzy and sickly.

Later that morning, Stuart turned up. "What has he done to you, Catherine, and why?"

"How did you know I was here?"

"I just saw Ruth in the shopping centre, and she told me you were in this hospital. So, what has Donald done to you?"

"Nothing. It was a nasty accident, but I am all right. No broken bones, just concussion. It was nothing to do with Donald; it was all my fault."

"I don't believe you. Does he know about the night of the party?"

"I swear to you, Stuart, I will never speak of that night. I swear that it was all my fault. Donald had nothing to do with the accident, but thank goodness he brought me to hospital. He is in a very distressed state. He must be reliving Christine's riding accident. I know what that is like. I need to get home to the manor, to Donald."

"You know I don't believe Christine's accident was an accident. I believe that Donald was responsible for it. Christine was going to leave him. I worry over your safety. Are you sure you are all right?"

"Yes. You should not listen to rumours about Donald's first wife." Then I stopped. "Oh my God! It was you, wasn't it? Christine was leaving Donald for you! Does Donald know?"

"Please, I spoke out of turn. I should not have said anything to you. I am just so worried about what Donald might do if he ever found out about us. And no, Donald does not know I am the person Christine was leaving him for. Please, please, do not let anyone know what I have told you."

I was shocked. "You hold the highest position on Donald's estate. Why did you continue to be employed by him?"

"I don't know. I just carried on. I met Jonathan, and we made a life for ourselves. Everything just became a memory."

"You should show Donald more respect. Don't worry. I will never speak of this. Now we have two secrets to keep."

Just then Ruth walked in with some clothes for me and, of course, her phone.

"Catherine, if you need me, please call," Stuart said. "Here is my card. I am always here for you." Then he left.

"Why do you need clothes?" asked Ruth. "What the hell has happened to you?"

I explained, very briefly, what had happened, and then I asked her to bring the Internet up on her phone. I talked her through the log-in to my email account. "Look for an email from Virgin Airlines. I received it before last Christmas, when we were living at the hotel."

As Ruth search through my emails, I put on the clothes she had bought. No underwear, but at least what she had fit me all right.

At last she found the message. I asked her to read it out to me. As I thought, the ticket was now four months out of date. "Right. Forward this to Donald's e mail address and place this message in it from me." I said. *"You bloody stupid man! Read the flight coupon and note that it is four months out of date. I had totally forgotten purchasing it. I did so on Justin's instructions, so that when I was ready I could fly out to look at Thomas's resting place. Justin offered to purchase my return fight. You bloody stupid man! Are you that insecure? I am on my way home! "*

Ruth sent the email and then helped me to finish dressing.

"They say that I have to wait for the consultant to discharge me," I told her. "I will wait a little while longer, and then we are going regardless. I want you to take me home. Don't worry about the things Donald has sent to the hotel. Someone will collect them tomorrow. I feel like I could hit him. I am so angry with him. Ruth, I hope I can rely on your discretion?"

Ruth assured me that she would not talk about what was happening.

The nurse came in and changed the dressing on my head. She was most insistent that I not leave until I was discharged.

It was nearly teatime. I had had enough of waiting. I told Ruth to find a wheelchair for me. She did. I immediately sat in it, and Ruth pushed it straight into the lift.

Once we were at her car, I sat in the passenger seat and Ruth took the wheelchair back. Then we set off for the manor. I had no key, and I knew that Babs would have gone home by then.

I needn't have worried. William, Donald's mate, was leaving as we pulled up at the main entrance. "Leave the door, William!" I shouted and got out of the car.

"Catherine, Donald has been drinking."

I told him not to worry and to go home. I told Ruth to leave me. After a deep breath, I went into the entrance hall.

It was obvious that Donald was in the lounge, so I made my way there. I staggered in, dizzy and most unwell. Donald looked startled. I fell into one of the sofas. "Have you read the email I sent not long ago?"

"No?" answered Donald.

"Read it now!" I screamed at him. "I said read it *now*!"

Donald stood by his desk. With his finger, he opened his iPad and pressed his email icon. I watched as he read. He looked up at me. "I don't know what to say. I misunderstood the situation. It still does not alter the fact that

I could have killed you. I could not cope with you being injured, and all the memories it brought back of Christine's accident. I am totally lost. So many dreadful things have happened to us. I have had enough." He was sobbing.

"Now you listen to me! All that matters from now on are you and I. I love you more than I have ever loved anybody. Did you hear that? I caused the accident when I lost control."

"So what do we do now? You know how much I love you. I know that I cannot live without you. What do you want me to do?"

"Don't you ever evict me again! Tomorrow you arrange for all my things to be collected from the hotel and brought back here. I want them put back *exactly* where they came from. Right now, I want you to carry me upstairs to our bedroom. I don't suppose you have noticed how I look? I feel bloody awful. There is no way I can get up those stairs myself."

Donald knelt down beside me and said, "You look terrible and your clothes look even worse. Mind you don't start to let yourself go." We laughed. He kissed my swollen cheek and put his head against my breast. I put my arms around him. I could feel his sobs.

"Come on, please carry me upstairs now," I said softly. "Lie with me until I fall asleep. I want to know that when I wake, you will be by my side. I need you more than ever now, and you need me."

Donald lifted me off the sofa and carried me upstairs. I kissed his face and neck and ran my fingers through his hair.

Once in the bedroom, he placed me under the covers and lay by my side, his arms holding me tight. "I love you so much, my beautiful Catherine with the swollen face. I will even try to get to know Sir Arthur."

"He has gone now. He will never return. Funny, but I have missed him," I said thoughtfully.

We kissed and stroked each other for reassurance. Then I whispered, "I know what you need to do, and that is to forgive but not to forget."